SPOOKY STORIES No. 4

"Go back! Go back!" howled Matt
uselessly against the wind. He began to
scramble down from the cave-mouth...but
a dark figure was now approaching. It
came swiftly forward, no more than a
shadow against the blackness—until, with
the suddenness of a lightning flash,
moonlight broke through the scudding sea-
wreck. For a moment it cast the beach into
glittering relief: Carrin's father lying on the
sand, weeping; the doused lantern; the
gaunt figure of a man, clad in unfamiliar
clothes and striding swiftly towards the
cave, towards *him,* his eyeballs catching
the moon-flash like cold fire....

From *Echoes in the Sand* by Roger F.
Dunkley, just one of the chilling tales to be
found within the fourth collection of
SPOOKY STORIES.

You may also enjoy these ghostly collections:

SPOOKY STORIES NO. 2
SPOOKY STORIES NO. 3
THE BEST OF SHADOWS
THE TISWAS BOOK OF GHASTLY GHOSTS

All published by CAROUSEL BOOKS

SPOOKY STORIES
NO. 4

Edited by Barbara Ireson
Illustrated by Daniel Woods

A CAROUSEL BOOK

TRANSWORLD PUBLISHERS LTD.

SPOOKY STORIES No. 4

A CAROUSEL BOOK 0   552   52201   5

First published in Great Britain by Carousel Books

PRINTING HISTORY
Carousel edition published 1982

Collection copyright © 1982 Barbara Ireson
Illustrations copyright © 1982 Transworld Publishers Ltd.

Carousel Books are published by
Transworld Publishers Ltd.,
Century House, 61–63 Uxbridge Road,
Ealing, London W5 5SA.

Made and printed in Great Britain by Cox Wyman Ltd., Reading.

ACKNOWLEDGEMENTS

ECHOES IN THE SAND by Roger F. Dunkley.
Copyright © Roger F. Dunkley 1980. First published in
Ghost Stories by Octopus Books Ltd.

THE WOODSEAVES GHOSTS by Catherine Gleason
Copyright © Catherine Gleason 1976.

THE OWL ON THE LEDGE by Genevieve Hawkins.
Copyright © Genevieve Hawkins 1980.

MISTY by Margaret Biggs
Copyright © Margaret Biggs 1978.

LONELY BOY by Paul Dorrell
Copyright © Paul Dorrell 1980. First published in
Ghost Stories by Octopus Books Ltd.

THE SINISTER SCHOOLMASTER by Rosemary
Timperley
Copyright © Rosemary Timperley 1978.

THREE GHOSTS by John Keir Cross
Copyright © John Keir Cross

CONTENTS

ECHOES IN THE SAND

by *Roger F. Dunkley*

'Matt's scared!'

Matt paused at the entrance to the cave.

Outside, the sun spilled down on the beach, topping the breaking waves with white fire. Inside was a twilight world, curving upwards into moist, rocky blackness. A seagull wailed mournfully overhead.

'He *is*! He's scared!' shouted Ben. He called to their sister, who was hesitantly teasing a crab in a nearby rock pool. 'Look, Maggie. Matt doesn't want to come into the cave.' Ben strode boldly into the dark mouth gashed in the cliff. His scornful

9

laugh took on a hollow ring as the mouth swallowed him.

He took several more steps and the darkness wrapped round him. He disappeared from view.

Matt hesitated. It was hard being the elder brother. You felt so responsible all the time. The cave might be dangerous; there could be rock falls and so on. And they were a long way from the village. What if anything happened to them? He looked back across the stretch of shining sand which formed the floor of the cove and saw the sharp, towering rocks over which they'd climbed to get here. They began to look like a wall which had shut them in.

Maggie, small and insistent, was tugging at his hand. 'Come on, Matt, let's explore,' she said, and ran off into the cave mouth.

'No!' shouted Matt suddenly, and surprised himself by the sharpness of his voice. 'Come back.'

'Coward!' boomed Ben's voice out of the darkness, followed by a hollow giggle from Maggie.

Matt stepped reluctantly out of the sunlight into the instant gloom of the cave. He shivered. It had a wet, cold smell. He waited for a moment, then groped a little further and stumbled against a rock. He put out a hand to support himself. He felt something warm, something that moved. His heart raced.

'Ouch!' said the something.

'Maggie!' Matt's voice betrayed his relief. '*There* you are!'

'There's no need to pinch,' said his sister, rubbing her arm in the gloom. 'Spooky, isn't it!' She shuddered, only half pretending.

'I *told* you to stay outside,' said Matt.

'Just because I'm younger than you....'

'No.... But if you're frightened....'

'*I'm* not frightened.'

'All right. Let's go and find Ben.'

Maggie hesitated. 'No,' she said uneasily.

'Well, go *back* then,' said Matt, exasperated.

'Shan't.'

Then she screamed. From the depths of the cave bubbled a dreadful laugh. Its echoes danced on the invisible surfaces around them.

'I'm going,' wailed Maggie.

She went.

Matt laughed. 'Ben!' he called. 'You shouldn't tease her like that. Where are you?'

'Here,' said the distant voice not very helpfully. 'It comes into a sort of cavern. But the tunnel gets jolly narrow first.'

Matt slithered forward with his head down, groping from sand to stones, from stones to rocks, until he felt the roof of the tunnel rising and found he could stand up again in safety.

He looked round. The darkness had been replaced by a grey light which hung in the cavernous space. Walls arched up and up like those of a cathedral. A thin beam of sunlight had found its way through a cleft in the rocks and kindled the white stalactites which dripped glittering from the roof.

'Wow!' said Matt, awed. A little booming 'Wow' came back from the surrounding walls.

Ben clambered off a nearby rock. 'Let's go,' he said, sounding less cheerful than before.

'Hang on,' said Matt. He put his head on one side. 'Can you hear anything?'

Ben shivered slightly and tried to disguise it by jumping up and down and rubbing his arms.

'*Now* who's scared?' said Matt, unable to resist

the taunt.

'Oh, come *on*,' said Ben.

'O-o-n. O-o-n,' sounded the cave on a curious booming note.

'No, wait a minute,' said Matt. 'It reminds me of something.'

Wasn't there some story…? he thought, and then remembered. An old saint.…Yes. St Nestan. Hundreds of years ago. People said he used to ring a bell when ships got too near the coast—or something like that. But what had it got to do with the cave?

'Hallo,' said Matt experimentally.

'Lo.…Lo.…Lo.…' murmured the cave.

'Oh, Matt,' said Ben, beginning to sound really frightened, 'you're not going to do your werewolf thing? Not here?'

Matt was tempted, but thought better of it. 'I just thought I'd heard a sort of…bell,' he said.

'Bell?' said Ben uneasily.

'Yes, bell. You know. A thing that goes ding-dong in a belfry.'

Ben saw that Matt was making a joke of it and felt better. 'Bats in the belfry!' he shouted. 'Matt's bats!' He laughed.

The sound broke the spell. Matt chased Ben cautiously back the way they had come, slithering and scrambling together, until they emerged again into the dazzling roar of surf and sunshine. He gave his younger brother a friendly thump.

Maggie was making letters in the sand just outside the cave. Ben, not looking where he was going, trod on them. Maggie howled. Matt dropped to his heels beside her. 'The sea would have spoiled them anyway,' he said. 'Look. The tide's nearly up to us.' He quickly scrawled letters in the sand: THIS IS MAGGIE NEWPORT'S BEACH. SEA, KEEP OFF.

In a moment water swirled round his ankles and then retreated, leaving a large blob and the words, THIS IS MAGGIE. Maggie giggled.

Ben joined in the game and scrawled, BEN WAS HERE, with a stick.

Typical! thought Matt. No imagination. He remembered the cave again and wondered whether his own imagination had led him astray. There had seemed to be a sound.... Like a bell.

Waves came up the beach and obliterated BEN. The three retreated.

'Are these yours?' said Matt presently, pointing to three crosses firmly etched in the sand.

'No,' said Maggie.

'Of course not,' said Ben scornfully, scrawling BEN IS STILL HERE with his finger. 'Catch *me* drawing kisses!'

Water washed away BEN for the second time and then retreated, leaving the sand fresh and bare—except for three crosses.

'Well, look at that,' said Ben indignantly.

Water washed round his ankles again, and again fell back. Three crosses remained.

'That's odd,' said Matt. He knelt down and swept the crosses away with his hand.

Again the tide swirled round their feet and ran back down the beach. Three crosses had reappeared.

Matt saw that Maggie was delighted and Ben merely puzzled, but the hairs on the back of his neck felt ruffled as though someone was watching him. He glanced over his shoulder at the mouth of the cave, but it was black and empty.

'I expect there are some rocks or something

underneath the sand,' he said. 'Maybe they make the water run like that.'

But as though to disprove him, the crosses had disappeared when the next wave swept their feet.

'Ding-dong,' said Ben, looking up from the tea-table with his mouth full of bread and butter. 'Matt's going mental, you know.'

'Serviette, dear,' said Mrs Newport absently.

'He's hearing things. *And* seeing crosses in the sand.'

Matt kept a dignified silence.

'I saw them, too,' said Maggie, spraying crumbs. 'Kisses. Crosses.'

'We *all* saw them,' said Matt quietly.

'We didn't all hear your ding-dong in the bel-frey.'

'I can't think what you're talking about, dear,' said Mrs Newport.

'Matt,' said Ben. 'He's bats in the belfrey. Batty Matty. Matty batty.'

'For goodness sake, Ben,' said Mrs Newport, watching Matt scowl and feeling some sympathy, 'do be your age. Thank heaven your father's coming down.'

The remark was well-judged. Matt beamed with satisfaction at the thought that somebody else could now take 'those kids' in hand. Maggie yelled. Ben shouted, 'When?'

'On Friday, dear. Don't shout. He 'phoned this afternoon. He's coming for the last weekend of the holiday.'

'The boat!' squeaked Maggie. 'Did Daddy say he'd take us out? In the new boat?'

'"Cruiser",' said Ben, 'not "boat". Mum, it's not fair. It's been tied up there by the jetty all holiday.

I could have navigated. Dad said so. It's not fair.'

'No, yes, no, no,' said Mrs Newport, trying to answer everybody's questions at once. 'I mean, I'm sure he'll take you out. If,' she added with quite unconvincing cunning, 'you behave very nicely for the rest of the week.'

Matt smiled quietly to himself. He knew that nothing would stop dad from showing off the new motor-vessel to the family as soon as he could.

Ben let out a noisy whoop of joy and skated about on the polished stone floor.

'Can Carrin come, too?' asked Maggie.

'Of course,' said Mrs Newport. 'Who's Carrin?'

'His dad's a fisherman,' said Ben. 'Grumpy old bloke. They live in those cottages at the end of the harbour.'

'They're lovely cottages,' said Mrs Newport. 'A bit pokey, though.'

'I think they're rather poor,' said Matt. "We met Carrin down the harbour.'

'You should've seen his jersey!' said Maggie. 'All holes. I don't think he's got a mum.'

'He was sitting staring at Dad's new boat. You could see he was dying for a ride in it. We couldn't see the harm in offering.'

'Of course not, dear.'

'But you should have seen his old man!' said Ben.

Matt nodded and raised his eyebrows. 'He growled something about flashy boats and rich trippers. Us, trippers!'

'Ah, well,' said Mrs Newport gently, 'anybody who comes down just for the summer must look like trippers to hard-working fishermen.'

Later, when Ben and Maggie had gone off to play smugglers and wreckers in the garden, she turned unexpectedly serious. 'What's this cave they're talking about?' she asked.

Matt explained. 'It's just up the coast,' he said. 'About a kilometre north of the village.'

'Near Trebarwitt?'

'Yes.'

Mrs Newport stood looking out of the kitchen window for a few moments.

'Matt,' she said presently, 'I don't want to be a spoil-sport or anything, but....'

'But what, Mum?'

'I think I'd rather you didn't all go back there again.'

'You're going to tell me it's haunted!' said Matt, managing to sound scornful but finding that his neck was prickling a little.

'Oh, *that*. Yes. Practically everything's haunted round here—you know what Cornish people are like! First of all there's that legend of St Nestan, saving ships with a bell or something. Then—if I've got the right cave—there are stories of terrible wails on stormy nights; shadowy shapes; a madman with eyes of fire prowling through the tunnels; and all that sort of thing.'

'Do you believe that, Mum?'

'No,' said Mrs Newport firmly.

'Well, then....?'

'There's something else,' she said, closing the kitchen door. 'Don't talk about it to the younger ones, but there's some story of a murder there. Something to do with wreckers and a man called Jack Fairmill.'

'*Wreckers*, Mum?' said Matt scornfully. 'There haven't been any wreckers since....Oh, I don't know. At least a hundred years.'

Through the window they could see Ben stand-

16

ing on a little mound, waving a bicycle lamp. Maggie, a sailing-ship in distress, ran to and fro with terrible moans. Presently, like a moth drawn to a candle, she stumbled against the mound and fell at Ben's feet, looking up at the lamp. 'I'm wrecked! I'm wrecked!' she wailed.

'I've lured her to your doom!' shouted Ben.

'He's lured her to her doom!' said Matt. 'Honestly! Where does he get it from?'

'Late Night Horror Movie, I should think,' said Mrs Newport. 'But I'm not sure the wreckers have gone, you know,' she went on. 'Remember that mysterious shipwreck up near Trebarwitt last year? Not far from that cave of yours. I'd much rather you didn't take Ben and Mags back there.'

'Okay, Mum. But who's Jack Fairmill?'

'I don't know, darling. Something to do with a murder, though. Perhaps he was a wrecker. You could ask that funny old Mr Oakes up at the Rectory. He's writing a book about the village.'

'You'll have to come back this afternoon,' said Mr Oakes' housekeeper suspiciously. 'And *only* this afternoon, mind. He's away up to Truro tomorrow. What'll I say you'm wanting?'

Matt hesitated. He had too many questions. He thought for a moment. 'I'd like to ask him about Jack Fairmill,' he said.

'Jack the Killer?' said the old woman with a harsh laugh. 'That's a big question, my son.'

Matt was told to come back at four that afternoon. 'Sharp, mind. He's a busy old owl, is the master.' She shut the door firmly.

The Rectory lay on the north side of the village. It was half way to the cave....

'Jack the Killer,' said Matt to himself with a

shudder. 'Wreckers. Murder.' What business was it of his? he wondered. Why not go straight home? But he found his feet turning towards the north. Twenty minutes later he had scrambled down the cliff path into the hidden cove.

Near the cave entrance Matt found what he was looking for and then wished that he hadn't.

The tide had been in twice since he was last here. Twice. It should have washed the beach quite clean. And yet....

He looked again to make sure.

In the smooth sand at the foot of the cave entrance there were the faint outlines of three crosses.

Matt lifted his foot, meaning to wipe them away but was stopped by a shrill laugh from somewhere above his head. He looked up, his heart pounding. A seagull swooped away.

He began to walk slowly backwards down the beach, not liking to turn his back on the cave, and then stumbled on a rock and fell. A clammy tentacle of seaweed slithered across his cheek. Matt turned and ran.

'You're scared!' he said to himself five minutes later, standing on the cliff top. 'Just plain scared!' Nothing, he felt, would make him go back to the little cove again. Nothing.

Perhaps not scared, he thought presently, walking back to the village. Perhaps just sensible. Perhaps it was only commonsense to keep away from a place like that; there might be rock falls or something.

But he knew that something important had happened. The crosses said so. He felt they were meant for him. He *had* to find out whatever Mr Oakes could tell him. It suddenly seemed urgent.

Mr Newport arrived at lunchtime, a day earlier than expected. Matt could see from the gleam in his eye that nothing would keep him off the water for very long. 'Oh, dear,' he thought, 'I'm going to have to choose between Dad and Mr Oakes. Why is everything so complicated?'

The lunchtime dishes were still on the table when Ben and Maggie started their war-dance round Father's chair.

'The boat! The boat!' chanted Maggie.

'The *cruiser*!' shouted Ben.

'Don't shout,' shouted Father.

'What on earth's all this shouting?' bellowed Mother.

'You promised,' wailed Maggie, 'And we promised Carrin.'

'Please! You've deafened the goldfish,' said Father.

'We haven't got any goldfish,' objected Maggie.

'I expect they left because of the noise,' said Father.

Silence arrived abruptly.

'Well, you might have the decency to laugh at my jokes if you want me to do you a favour,' said Mr Newport.

'What jokes?' said Ben, and ducked.

His father cuffed him playfully. 'When do we set sail, bo's'n?' he asked. 'Any objections to this afternoon?'

'Wowee!' said Ben.

'I suppose…' said Matt hesitantly, and then thought better of it.

'What?'

'Dad, I don't think I can come with you this afternoon.'

'Why on earth not?' said Mr Newport. 'I don't

see much of you, Matt…. And I thought you were pleased about the new boat.'

'Oh, I am, Dad,' said Matt. 'It's just that….'

Mr Newport shrugged and tried not to look put out. 'If you've something better to do, of course.'

'I'm sorry, Dad.'

Ben and Maggie rushed away to put their sea-clothes on. 'Poor old Matt,' shouted Ben over his shoulder. 'Afraid of being seasick, I expect. Batty Matty. Seasick Matty.'

Matt remained, staring gloomily out of the window.

'You've really disappointed your father,' said Mrs Newport in a cross whisper.

'Damn!' said Matt miserably. 'Damn! Damn!' He went out, giving the door a little slam.

'Well, really,' said Mr Newport, raising his eyebrows. 'How long has he been like this?'

'It's his age, I expect,' said Mrs Newport. 'You know how they get.'

Outside, the Rectory was smothered with ivy; inside, it was smothered with books and papers.

'Well, now. Well, now. What now?' hooted Mr Oakes, perching his small, grey-flannel body on the edge of the desk. He peered at Matt through large, bright eyes which were magnified by thick glasses. He looked like a little owl which had accidentally grown a moustache.

'We've done old St Nestan, boy. What do you want to know now?'

There had not been much more to learn about St Nestan. Matt was almost disappointed. Centuries ago, Mr Oakes had said, some old hermit had lived in a cave or a hole in this part of Cornwall. People called him St Nestan. He had spent his life, when he wasn't fasting or praying, trying to stop shipwrecks. 'Walked about on the beach with a lamp and a big bell,' said Mr Oakes. 'Must have looked a proper sight, ho, ho! Just like a little lighthouse!'

'What about the bell?' asked Matt.

'Never been seen, boy. But they say it used to ring sometimes. In the days of the wreckers. Must have had a guardian angel. Or some old madman. Ho, ho!'

'When did the wreckers stop?' said Matt.

Mr Oakes turned solemn. His eyes grew wide and owlish. 'That's a *history* question, boy. I'm only writing legends, you know. Ask me something else.'

Matt had the feeling that Mr Oakes was not telling him all he knew. He thought about the crosses in the sand. 'What do three X's mean?' he asked, feeling rather foolish.

Mr Oakes looked quite excited. 'Wha—a—at a good question!' he hooted, flapping his arms. 'Sounds like folklore. Or a secret code. Or an ancient language. Could be children being naughty, of course.'

'No,' said Matt.

'Let me see, now. Kisses?'

'No.'

'A winning line in a football pool?'

'No.'

'Hmmmm!' said Mr Oakes. 'Haaaa! What about a Roman thirty? XXX, you know.'

'Oh,' said Matt. 'Thirty what?'

'Ho—o—ow should I know?' hooted Mr Oakes indignantly. 'That's your problem, boy.' He waved his arms about, scattering papers like feathers. 'Any *more* questions?' he added.

21

Matt had a question but was nervous about asking it. Looking out of the study window, he was surprised to see that the afternoon had turned windy and overcast. Low clouds were scudding across the sky.

'Well, now. What now?' prompted Mr Oakes.

'Jack the Killer…' began Matt hesitantly, listening to a mutter of thunder in the distance.

'Who—o—o—o?' screeched Mr Oakes, jumping up from the desk. A little burst of wind hurled raindrops against the study windows.

'Jack Fairmill,' said Matt. 'Why do they call him "Jack the Killer"?'

Suddenly Mr Oakes seemed large and angry. He puffed up his chest and widened his eyes until they seemed enormous. 'Whooooo's been telling you tales, boy? Who—o—o? Who—o—o?' For a moment the moustache looked like a little beak.

'I'm sorry, sir,' said Matt, leaning back from Mr Oakes' wagging forefinger and slipping in 'sir' as a precaution.

Mr Oakes relented a little. His ruffled feathers began to subside. 'I'm writing a chapter about Jack Fairmill,' he hooted, flapping an arm at the desk and sending papers scurrying. 'You'll have to wait for my book, boy. But I'll tell you this…'

'Yes?' said Matt uneasily.

'Jack Fairmill lived about a hundred and fifty years ago. When the wreckers were at their worst. And he was quite mad, you know. Ma—a—a—ad!'

'Yes, sir,' said Matt meekly.

'But he *disappeared*!' said Mr Oakes with a chirping shriek. 'There isn't a trace of him after 1840. Not a gravestone, not a cross, not even a line in the parish register.'

'But…what did he kill?'

'Aaaa—a—ah! That's a question! What indeed, boy?' Mr Oakes settled his head between his shoulders with a hunched look. The eyes blinked. 'You'll have to wait for that book of mine,' he said. 'But I'll tell you two things more. Some of the villagers know more than they like to tell. And….'

'And….?'

'There's still a Fairmill or two living in these parts.'

'But.'

'But you ask too many questions, boy. You'll have to buy my book. And now you'd better fly home. There's quite a storm coming. I can feel a storm from ten kilometres away, you know.'

As Matt left, Mr Oakes was ruffling through his papers again. One or two drifted idly to the floor, like leaves or feathers in the first, small eddies of an approaching gale.

Matt ran home through the gathering dusk. It was now far too stormy to go down to the jetty to meet Dad, as he had thought of doing.

From the lane which led down to the cottage he was surprised to see three figures silhouetted against the sky on the coast road further up the hill. They were trudging north, heavily clad in waterproofs. One of them seemed to have a large, unlighted lantern. He looked a little like Carrin's father, though it was impossible to be sure in the bad light.

As Matt came into the kitchen he could hear his mother talking on the telephone. She sounded anxious. 'Yes…,' she was saying. 'Yes….But I want to be there to meet them….Yes, I *know* it could be a long wait….'

Matt put his head round the door.

'Oh, darling,' said Mrs Newport, putting the 'phone down, 'I'm just going down to the harbour. Dad's a bit late back with the boat. They think he's been held up by the storm.'

'I'll come, too, Mum.'

'I'd rather you stayed here, darling. In case there's a 'phone message—from up the coast, or something. You can ring me at the jetty if you hear....'

'It's okay, Mum,' said Matt firmly. 'I'm sure it's okay. I'll bake some spuds in their jackets for when you all get home.'

'Oh, Matt,' said Mrs Newport, kissing him lightly on the forehead, 'you're so like Dad some-times.'

She went out, and he presently heard the car drive away into the wind and the rain.

Looking out of the window, Matt saw that the storm was worsening. It was driving hard towards the north—towards Trebarwitt, towards....An image of the cave rose to his mind. He thought of Dad's cruiser, perhaps also drifting towards the north. He thought of three men, silhouetted against the skyline, trudging north....carrying a lantern....

He wandered about the living-room, restless and uneasy. Everything seemed to be happening at once—today. He suddenly caught his breath as the calendar on Mum's writing-table leapt to his eye.

It was the thirtieth of August.

The thirtieth.

Thirty.

XXX.

Three crosses in the sand.

Someone or something had given him a message. It meant, 'Now! Today!'

'Oh, no!' said Matt out loud. 'Oh, please, not me.'

But already he was pulling on the great, thick sweater and the heavy oilskin which Dad had bought him at the beginning of the summer, when anything so thick and heavy seemed absurd, and the sunshine looked as if it would last forever.

Carrin stood next to Mr Newport in the wheelhouse of the cruiser. Spray lashed against the glass enclosure and the boat rocked and plunged alarmingly, in the heavy sea. They had been out of sight of land for nearly three hours.

'Where do you reckon we are?' said Mr Newport. He was a good navigator, but the freak storm had thrown them far off course. It was a comfort to have a local fisherman's son with him.

Carrin peered into the cloudy seascape ahead, but for the moment said nothing.

'Dad!' shouted Ben excitedly from behind Carrin's shoulder, 'there's a light! Look. Can't you see it?'

A tiny flicker was visible from dead ahead.

'It's land all right,' said Mr Newport. 'Could be the jetty beacon.'

Carrin narrowed his brown eyes with an uncertain expression. 'Reckon it's too far north,' he said. 'There's terrible rocks round Trebarwitt. Reckon you'd better go south a while.'

'But the *light*,' said Ben. 'It must be the harbour or something.'

Carrin shrugged, dropping his eyes. 'Can't be sure of nothing,' he said.

'Well,' said Mr Newport, 'I think we'd better

head for the light for a while. It's the only thing I've got to steer by.'

Matt's heart was pounding as he stumbled down the last few metres of the cliff path towards the cove. Coming out from behind a rocky shoulder, he stopped dead and held his breath. Barely seven metres away, with their backs turned to him, were three men clad in heavy oilskins. One of them was holding a lighted lantern on a tall pole. It carried a large reflector, pointing out to sea. Though the wind was howling, snatches of the men's rapid talk gusted back to where Matt stood.

'Rich all right…' The voice was that of Carrin's father's. 'That good-for-nothing lad of mine.…I've made him keep an eye on 'em.…There's rich pickings there.…'

'…that lad o' yours?' said another voice with an unpleasant laugh. 'Needs a thrashing, that one.…Proper little softie.…got it from his mother, I wouldn't wonder.…'

'…you can lay off that kind o' talk.…' Carrin's father again, loud and angry.

'She were a Fairmill, weren't she?' A third voice this time, high-pitched and sneering.

The lantern swayed as Carrin's father swung round and shook his fist. 'Never you mind what she were!' he shouted. 'She were a good wife till she died.' The rest was swept away by the wind.

The four men fell silent.

Four men?

Matt counted them again. Carrin's father, holding the lantern. Two companions to the left of him. But now—a few paces behind them stood another figure. A ragged and shadowy man with a tattered shirt and torn breeches.

Matt's teeth began to chatter. He had a violent impulse to turn tail and run. But he knew what he must now do. With his heart racing and his stomach muscles knotted, he began to creep slowly forward. To his right, the mouth of the cave had now come into view.

'We'd better keep going,' said Mr Newport, holding his voice steady and staring straight ahead.

He saw suddenly with shock that tears were running down Carrin's face. 'What is it?' he said angrily. It was bad enough trying to keep Mags and Ben cheerful without having to cope with a fisherman's son who ought to know better than to start crying at a little wind and rain.

'Da' couldn't have known,' said Carrin in a choked voice. 'He couldn't have known.'

'Known what?'

'That his own son.... That I... was on this boat. That's a wrecker's light, Mr Newport! Mr Newport, please save us! Turn back!'

'For heaven's sake, boy,' said Mr Newport angrily. 'Stop talking nonsense and pull yourself together. Fine fisherman's lad *you* are! You're frightening the younger ones.'

There *was* something wrong with that light, though. And there were some rocks to starboard which shouldn't have been there.

But they'd better keep going, thought Mr Newport. What else was there to do in the stormy darkness, with fuel running low and little to be seen except that flickering beacon?

Mr Newport steered ahead.

The mouth of the cave yawned and swallowed Matt alive. The back of his neck was prickly with risen hairs.

The four men were still in view: three wreckers and one, silent and apart.

Behind him the cave moaned and boomed as a gust of wind swept into it. Further back, the main cavern reverberated with a deep, ominous note.

Matt knew that the time had come. He dared not wait any longer. He took a deep breath and then shouted with all his might.

'The curse of St Nestan!' he screamed into the wind. 'The curse of St Nestan be upon you!' His words were magnified by the rocky tunnel. Their echoes were taken up by the great cavern behind him. 'Nestan! Nestan! Nestan!' shrieked the cave like a giant in agony.

The three wreckers spun round. They seemed to look right through the fourth man without seeing him. Carrin's father stood stock still, holding the lantern. The other two began to run towards the mouth of the cave.

'Jack Fairmill!' shouted Matt on a sudden impulse. 'Behind you. Look. Jack Fairmill. Jack the Killer!'

The two men stopped; turned; looked about them; began to retreat. Matt could have sworn that one of them stumbled through the strange fourth figure.

'Where? Where?' shouted one.

'What in God's name?' came the high-pitched voice of the other.

'Superstitious fools!' yelled Carrin's father. 'It's only some filthy brat. Look. Up there. In Nestan's Hole. Drag the little devil out!' But his companions had already vanished into the blackness like snuffed candles, their voices dying on the wind.

Carrin's father, lantern held aloft, began to tread menacingly up the beach. 'I'll see for you, my sonny!' he roared.

'Carrin! Carrin! Carrin!' shrieked Matt.

Carrin's father halted, peering uncertainly ahead.

'Carrin. He's on that boat. Carrin. Your son. He's on my father's boat!'

Carrin's father gave a terrible groan. 'God save us!' he said, dropping the lantern. He fell to his knees in the sand. 'God spare us! For the lad's mother.'

In the lampless gloom it seemed to Matt that the fourth figure was now standing over Carrin's father where he knelt weeping on the beach.

From somewhere out at sea the faint chug-chug of a motor-vessel could now be heard, faint or loud as the wind caught the distant sound and gusted it shorewards.

'Go back! Go back!' howled Matt uselessly against the wind. He began to scramble down from the cave-mouth....but a dark figure was now approaching. It came swiftly forward, no more than a shadow against the blackness—until, with the suddenness of a lightning flash, moonlight broke through the scudding sea-wreck. For a moment it cast the beach into glittering relief: Carrin's father lying on the sand, weeping; the doused lantern; the gaunt figure of a man, clad in unfamiliar clothes and striding swiftly towards the cave, towards *him*, his eyeballs catching the moon-flash like cold fire.

Matt gave a moan of terror and fled, stumbling, into the cave—back along the narrow tunnel, over the dank rocks and shifting sand, into the central cavern. Something brushed past him in the darkness like an icy wind.

Matt shrieked. The cavern resounded. Words seemed to form themselves in the choking blackness.

'Kill...' resounded the rocks. 'I'll kill....Let Fairmill kill....Oh, sweet Nestan!....Help Fairmill kill...their devilish trade....Before they kill...so many souls. Before they kill...poor Jack...poor Jack.'

Falling forward into a merciful unconsciousness, Matt heard the first, deep, tolling notes of a great bell. In the echo-chamber of the cavern they thundered upon him, driving him down into oblivion with hammer-blows of unbearable sound.

'The bell!' Carrin pointed urgently towards the shore. The wind tore at the notes calling into the night. 'Turn back!' he yelled. 'Listen! We *must* turn back.'

Suddenly, to starboard, a dark rock loomed from the water where no rock should have been. Waves pounded against it, lashing spray into the wind.

'Dear God!' exclaimed Mr Newport. On every side black shapes thrust out of the sea, teeth bared, ancient, hungry.

He struggled with the controls. The engine throbbed and protested; spray crashed against the wheelhouse; Maggie screamed as a rock lurched towards them out of the blackness. With a final heave, the wallowing vessel began to reverse towards the open sea.

Carrin shivered. 'That was St Nestan's bell,' he said.

At the end of the garden Ben and Maggie played at shipwrecks with Carrin in the September sunlight. 'Ding-dong! Ding-dong!' chanted Maggie, pretending to be a marker-buoy with a sea-bell. Ben glanced in Matt's direction, where he lay at ease in the deckchair, resting a bandaged leg. 'How d'you feel?' he asked.

'Sound,' said Matt, grinning, 'as a bell.'

'I still don't know how you had the strength to ring that thing,' said Mr Newport.

'But I didn't,' said Matt. 'I keep telling you.' He shook his head. How could he explain the inexplicable? An icy wind rushing past him in a dark cave.

'Jack the Killer!' he said with a little laugh. 'But all he tried to kill was the work of the wreckers. So I suppose that's why they killed *him*. Jack the Killed, really. Murdered—not a murderer. No wonder he haunted that cave!'

Mrs Newport shuddered. 'That's enough, Matt. No more hauntings, now.'

Matt looked thoughtful. 'D'you know, Mum? I think you're right: no more hauntings...now.'

He lay back, closing his eyes against the sun. He remembered one final incident from that strange night which he had not mentioned to anyone—and never would. Lying on the beach after Carrin's father had carried him from the cave, Matt had noticed something in the sand, now lit by peaceful moonlight. Three marks. Faint but unmistakable. They had seemed to appear one after the other. The first was a cross, but the others were letters: a P and an A.

XAP, they seemed to read, until one remembered what they would look like from the other side—from the direction of the cave.

PAX.

The Latin for 'Peace'.

THE WOODSEAVES GHOSTS

by Catherine Gleason

'The only snag about staying at Woodseaves,' said
David Mitchell, 'is the library.'

'Yes,' his sister Sally agreed. 'Do you remember
how frightened we were when we first saw it? We
were sure there were ghosts about, hiding in the
corners!'

'I'm not so sure that it isn't haunted,' said David,
with an air of mystery. Sally was two years younger
than him and she usually believed every word he
said.

Her eyes grew big as saucers. 'You don't really
think so, do you? What do you mean?'

'Well, you remember reading in that local history book about the boy and girl who were supposed to have disappeared in there? It was exactly a hundred and fifty years ago that they vanished. So they might turn up again.' His voice dropped to a whisper. 'One of these Fridays, when we're in the library doing our school work, the air will turn cold and the door will slowly start to open...creeeak...'

'Oh, stop it!' cried Sally. 'You're making me shiver!'

'And then,' continued David in a creepy voice, 'something dressed in a long white gown will glide in...and—grab you!'

Sally gave a little shriek and covered her ears, while David burst out laughing. 'Only teasing you, silly.'

'You are horrid, David,' said Sally, giggling in spite of herself. 'You're just trying to scare me because we have to do some work in there tonight. Well, I'm not afraid!'

'Neither am I, really,' said David. 'Come on, slowcoach, we're going to be late for tea. Where's Max?'

The heavy golden labrador lumbered up to them and they made their way back through Woodseaves Park to the Hall.

Great-Uncle Timothy Mitchell owned the Hall, and lived there with his housekeeper Martha and, of course, Max. Like his house, Uncle Tim was rather Victorian and rambling, but David and Sally were very fond of him and loved spending their summer holidays at Woodseaves.

This was the first year their parents hadn't been with them, because their father had taken a job in America that summer and Mrs Mitchell had gone with him.

Martha was very neat and motherly and precise, and she had been Uncle Tim's housekeeper for donkeys' years. She was only ever strict about one thing, and that was their doing an hour or so's work in the library on the subjects they hadn't done very well in at school. This, as David said, was the one snag about staying there, but then it wasn't much of a disadvantage, considering all the other things that Woodseaves had to offer. Midway between the town and the country, everything was within easy reach, from riding stables to a cinema.

'What did you do with yourselves today, children?' Uncle Tim asked them over tea.

He and Martha had always called David and Sally 'children', and David suspected that they always would, no matter how big they grew.

'We fed the goldfish in the pond, and then David climbed a tree and nearly fell in the stream, and then the Smithson twins took us over to South Meadow to see the lambs,' said Sally. 'They're getting quite big now.'

'What, the Smithsons?' The old man looked startled.

'No, Uncle, the lambs,' giggled Sally. Uncle Tim was so vague at times.

'I was reading about ghosts in a local history book,' said David. 'Do you know there are supposed to be two of them here at Woodseaves?'

'That's right.' Uncle Tim chuckled. 'A brother and his young sister, about the same ages as you two. They were said to have been murdered by their wicked step-mother, or some such nonsense.'

'Why?' demanded Sally, who had more than her fair share of curiosity.

'The stepmother wanted Woodseaves for her own sons, and the other two were in the way, I suppose.'

'Really, Mr Timothy, you shouldn't be filling the children's heads with such stories,' said Martha reprovingly. 'We've lived here more years than we care to remember, and we've never seen any ghosts.'

'That's probably because there aren't any such things,' suggested David.

'Exactly. Ghosts don't exist.'

Sally wasn't so sure.

'There. Finished at last.' David threw down his pen thankfully and stretched, pushing back his chair. It had taken him nearly an hour to plough through his French exercise.

'Well, hang on a minute,' said Sally crossly. She was struggling with a maths problem.

'O.K.' Idly, David glanced around the library. All the other rooms at Woodseaves were light and modern-furnished, but even in the height of summer the library looked gloomy, damp and ancient. Hundreds of old books, some very valuable, were shut into dark, glass-fronted cases against the walls, and the firelight cast weird dancing reflections on to them.

'Nearly finished now,' said Sally, one hand stroking Max, who shifted restlessly beside her. The big dog always seemed uneasy in the library. Suddenly he jumped up and ran over to the window, barking furiously.

'Max! Come and lie down,' ordered David.

Max slunk reluctantly away from the window, tail down, to the opposite corner of the room. He made a funny sort of noise, half way between a whine and a howl, and scratched at the door, looking back at them with piteous eyes. David opened the door for him and the dog shot out of the room as if something was after him.

'That's strange,' said Sally. 'Maybe he saw a cat outside?'

'I don't think so.' David peered out of the window at the dusky night. 'Perhaps he—'

Suddenly all the lights went out, and, except for the glowing fire, the room was plunged into darkness. Sally gave a little scream.

'It's all right,' said David calmly, sitting by the fire. 'The lights have fused, that's all. I expect Uncle will have them on again in a minute.'

'I hope so,' said Sally. 'It's rather scary in here with—oh!' She broke off with a cry of astonishment.

David swung round and followed her gaze to the window. His mouth dropped open in sheer amazement as he saw two strange figures, hand in hand, passing straight through the window into the library!

David and Sally clutched each other in terror. But the figures did not look terrifying; they were a boy and a girl, dressed in old-fashioned clothes.

'Do not be afraid. We are not come to harm you,' said the boy.

'What…who are you?' asked David in a quavery voice.

'My name is Lucretia, and this is my brother, Comus,' said the girl, with a slight bow.

'Er…how do you do,' said Sally, a little unsteadily.

'May we sit down? We have been wandering for many years, and we are somewhat fatigued,' the boy introduced as Comus said politely.

Sally rubbed her eyes and stared. The ghostly figures sat quite calmly in the two leather arm-chairs opposite and, through their outlines, she could see the chairs quite clearly.

'David,' she whispered, 'do you think we're dreaming?'

'No,' said David excitedly. 'I think they're the two who were murdered here—don't you remember Uncle Tim's story?—and they've come back to the—to the scene of the crime,' he finished lamely.

'Indeed, you are right,' said Lucretia in her sweet, light voice. 'Our lives were cut short very much against our wills, one hundred and fifty years ago this very evening.'

David nodded. 'Uncle Tim told us about you.'

Sally wriggled in her chair. Half of her was scared enough to dash straight out of the library, shrieking for Uncle Tim, but the other half was full of inquisitiveness. After a short struggle, curiosity won.

'How did it happen?' she asked finally. 'Your being murdered, I mean.'

'Yes, how?' David, too, was still a little frightened, and spoke rather more aggressively than he intended. 'Our uncle said you were killed by a wicked stepmother, like people in a fairy tale, and it all sounds very fishy to me.'

Comus and Lucretia looked at each other in a puzzled way.

'It had nothing to do with fish,' said Comus. 'It was poisoned veal, as I remember.'

'That is right,' said Lucretia. 'You see, our mama died when we were a little younger than you are now, and Papa married again, almost straight away. He was a very good man, and he

39

wished to secure a second mother for us.'

'But his second wife, our stepmother, was a most wicked woman,' continued Comus. 'She was widowed too, and she married Papa in order to provide for her own baby sons. Really, you know, she did not care a rap for him or for us. She only wanted her children to have Woodseaves, and we stood in the way, because Woodseaves would have been ours when we were old enough to inherit it.'

'At first, we did not realise the extent of her malice,' Lucretia resumed, 'though we did consider it odd when she told us that deadly nightshade was good for us, and to eat as much as we could if ever we found it growing wild.'

'And she was always suggesting that we go for a bathe in the deepest part of the river,' added Comus. 'After we told her repeatedly that we could not swim!'

'Yet she was always very pleasant to us,' Lucretia sighed. 'We hardly believed she could wish us any harm. Then, one evening, she served us a dish of veal here in the library where we were reading, and that was that.'

'You were poisoned?' asked Sally, round-eyed.

'Yes—we fell asleep, and awoke like this.' Comus held up a transparent hand.

'And what happened to your stepmother?' asked David.

'She died of the consumption shortly afterwards, and confessed on her deathbed to having poisoned us. Her sons did not long survive her, and so it was all a wasted effort, really.' Lucretia looked sadly into the fire.

'What a shame!' cried the warm-hearted Sally indignantly. 'I think it's terrible that you should have had such short, unhappy lives. Honestly,

David, we don't know how lucky we are, do we?'

'You're right,' agreed David seriously. 'We do have marvellous parents, when you come to think about it. None of this wicked-stepmother stuff at all.'

Comus and Lucretia exchanged glances of something like envy.

'Your parents, then, are very kind?' asked Comus wistfully.

'Oh, yes! They couldn't be nicer,' said Sally eagerly. 'I wish we could help you,' she added to their phantom visitors.

'Perhaps you can,' said Comus at once. 'For we have come here tonight to offer you a proposition.'

'What kind of proposition?' David asked suspiciously.

'We wish to change places with you,' said Comus simply. 'If you are agreeable to our suggestion, we would become you, and you would become—'

'Ghosts?' said Sally faintly.

'Er...I don't think we'd like that very much, thank you,' said David. 'Anyway, why us?'

'Why, because you are here at Woodseaves,' said Lucretia. 'And you are about the same ages as we are. Being a ghost can be great fun, you know,' she added mischievously. 'Watch me!'

And before their eyes, she vanished. David and Sally watched breathlessly as a heavy vase rose into the air, apparently by itself, and flew across the room. 'Catch!' came a gleeful cry from nowhere, and David had to go into a quick rugby dive to save the vase before it hit the ground.

There was a tinkling laugh and Lucretia appeared again. 'There! You see? Some very naughty ghosts do that sort of thing all the time.'

'I don't think we'd want to drift about chucking vases around, actually,' said Sally, as David rubbed his bruised elbows.

'Oh, dear!' sighed Lucretia.

'Perhaps you would prefer to reside in the celestial regions?' suggested Comus.

'What do you mean?' asked Sally. 'You do talk oddly, you know!'

'Everybody talked like that a hundred and fifty years ago,' David reminded her.

'Precisely. I beg your pardon,' Comus apologised to Sally. 'I meant to say, how about Heaven?'

And just then, the door opened.

'Are you still in here, children?' Martha fiddled with the light switch. 'Have both of the light bulbs gone? What a nuisance!' She came into the firelit room, glancing straight at the ghostly figures in the armchairs.

'We were just talking, Martha,' said Sally.

'Well, don't stay too long, dears. Bed in half an hour, you know.'

'Why didn't Martha see you?' asked David, as soon as she had gone.

'We did not wish her to,' said Comus.

'What was that you said about Heaven?' Sally demanded impatiently.

'My brother wondered if you would care to go there,' said Lucretia carelessly.

'Have you really been to Heaven? I don't believe it!' said David.

'Indeed we have,' said Lucretia, with indignation. 'We might have stayed there, too, but that we kept on hankering after life on earth, and THEY do not like it if you are half-hearted about Heaven. And so we came back. Won't you change places with us, please?' she asked imploringly.

'THEY wouldn't mind, you know.'

David and Sally did not ask who THEY were; they rather thought they knew already.

'Well, really, I don't think...' began David doubtfully, but Sally was overcome with curiosity and cut in with:

'What's it really like in Heaven? Do tell us all about it.'

'Oh, it is a wonderful place, of course, but much depends on whereabouts you go. There are many different sections,' explained Comus.

'How do you mean?' Sally was puzzled. Heaven was Heaven, wasn't it?

'Well,' said Lucretia, 'there is one part where all the soldiers go who have been killed in battle. They feast and drink all the time, and have their wounds bandaged. I found it monotonous—dull, you know,' she added, wrinkling her nose and tossing back her light brown ringlets. 'All of their conversation concerns war and battles. It is messy too, with all that blood and iodine.'

'Valhalla!' cried David excitedly. 'I've heard about that at school—it's the Heaven of the Vikings. Do all the Chinese Kung Fu fighters who get beaten go there as well?'

Comus looked puzzled. 'I have never heard of this Kung Fu,' he confessed. 'The Eastern people generally seem to go to Nirvana, where they do nothing but sit and think all the time. They call it meditation. Now that really is dull.'

'The Mount Olympus one is quite pleasant,' said Lucretia doubtfully. 'If you like hatching plots and chasing fauns through forests, that is. I believe they have a few unicorns and winged horses there, too.'

'Really? Winged horses?' Sally was thrilled. She

43

was pony-mad.

'Yes. And there is ordinary Heaven as well, where you walk on clouds and wear haloes,' said Comus. 'A great many Royal Air Force pilots seem to end up there. I think they really mean to go to Valhalla, but they cannot resist the wings, you see.'

'It also helps if you play a musical instrument,' added Lucretia. 'Won't you change places with us? I am sure you would like it very much.'

'How could you do that?' asked David curiously.

'Oh! That is very simple,' said Comus. 'We hold your hands for a second, and concentrate very hard, and our minds would change places with yours. You see? It is extremely easy.'

'Well—I'm really very sorry,' said David, 'but I'm afraid we can't.'

'No,' said Sally regretfully. 'It's our parents, you see. They would miss us terribly.'

'Ah, but they would never know,' argued Comus. 'After all, we would look exactly the same as you. It's just that we should have swapped minds. Within a few weeks we could learn to talk as you do, and then nobody at all would be able to tell the difference.'

'I'm afraid it's impossible,' said David slowly.

There was a sad little pause. Comus looked very downcast, and Lucretia dabbed her eyes with a transparent lace handkerchief. Sally thought longingly about unicorns and winged horses, and David tried very hard not to think of Valhalla.

'Well!' Comus said finally. 'Then there is nothing more to be said. We had better be going.'

'I'm so sorry we couldn't help,' said Sally, 'and it's been simply marvellous talking to you.'

'It has been our pleasure,' said Comus and Lucretia politely. 'We wish you goodnight.' And they

44

put out their hands in farewell.

'Goodbye,' said Sally and David, and without thinking they shook hands with the ghostly pair.

'Now then, children!' Martha pushed opened the library door. 'It really is getting late. Oh, good, the lights are working again. I've cooked you some fish fingers for a suppertime snack—come along to the kitchen before they get cold.' And she bustled out again.

They looked at each other and smiled.

'What on earth can fishes' fingers look like, Sister? Evidently a new variety of fish has been discovered.'

'Indeed; when we were here last, fish did not even have hands, let alone fingers. Let us go and try them!'

Hand in hand, they walked out of the library to find the kitchen.

LONELY BOY

by Paul Dorrell

Jimmie Edmonds wandered across the school courtyard and made his way to the green where the other boys were playing football. He hoped that today they might let him join in the game. Especially as he had a brand new ball, one of the very best.

What in fact happened was that Nick Clark, the form bully, snatched the ball from under his arm and knocked Jimmie over in the mud. Then they all ran off, laughing and calling him 'teacher's pet'. This was most unfair, because, although he *was* clever and *did* work hard, he had never, at least

47

not often, tried to 'suck up' to any of the teachers. It just happened that they liked his serious approach to school, wanted to encourage him; and they all felt a special sympathy with this shy boy who had lost his mother so recently. However hard he tried, Jimmie could not be as outgoing and carefree as the others of his age. But at thirteen most boys still have a great deal to learn about how other people think and feel. Jimmie's trouble was partly that he was just a bit more adult in his approach to life, this due largely to his recent bereavement and the amount of time which his father had always spent with him, encouraging him to be interested in all manner of serious subjects. And Mr Edmonds had instilled in his son a spirit of inquiry, made him challenge the ideas which he received from others and sought to make him understand why people acted as they did.

The mud clung to his hands and his clothes too hard for him to brush it off. He would have to take a bath when he arrived home, and wash his trousers. It was while he stood there, at the edge of the green, struggling to overcome the feeling of utter loneliness which seemed to engulf him, that he became aware of the curious gaze of another boy. He had not seen him approach, nor heard him, but now only a few metres separated them. There could not have been more than a few months difference in age either way between them. More than that, Jimmie felt some strange affinity with this newcomer, even though he had no idea who he was, had never seen him in town before. Ah! He looked as lonely as Jimmie himself was.

'Hello,' said the new boy, timidly.

It was a little while before Jimmie could answer.

They both stood staring at one another, totally oblivious of the others who were now at the far end of the green. There was something strange about the clothes and the haircut, decided Jimmie. Perhaps he was a foreigner. There were so many in England now, with the world in such a state. His father talked about politics sometimes, and, although he could not always seize the exact meaning of it all, he was no longer surprised at the strange people one saw.

'Hello. I'm Jimmie,' he said, suddenly finding a new self-confidence which was born partly of sympathy for the stranger. He held out his hand, and it was only then that he realized how withered and small was the arm which he had expected to see extended to him. He blushed at his clumsiness; he should have noticed!

'I'm sorry,' said the other. 'Something went wrong when I was born. They don't quite know what.' He smiled wanly. 'I don't get to play very much. Others boys say they don't want a cripple in their crowd.'

'They don't seem to like me much either,' replied Jimmie. 'Perhaps we'd better form our own team. Except I don't have my own ball any more.' He pointed to the players in the distance.

'We could go for a walk. I've got strong legs,' said the…

No, not a foreigner, decided Jimmie. At least, not judging from his accent. But what was it about him that was so strange? Apart from his clothes and haircut, there was nothing definite, just a…difference? Why worry about it? He had someone to spend time with now, and he need not be alone. And the other boy obviously felt the same way about Jimmie.

'Oh yes! My name's Tom Nicholson. My father's just taken over as manager at Simmonds' factory....' Obviously he had expected Jimmie to show some sign of recognition, but he did not push the point when he saw that this information meant nothing.

'Where would you like to go?' Jimmie asked.

'We could go up to the top of Reacher's Hill. They say there are the remains of an old Roman fort there.'

'So they say, but I've never been able to find anything. Still, it's a good walk—if that's really all right with you.' Jimmie looked at Tom with concern.

'As I said, I've got strong legs,' said Tom. 'You can always give me a hand—if you don't mind.' He laughed as he realized the irony of what he had just said, and this was so easy and natural to him that Jimmie was able to laugh too. When you're lonely and you find someone who doesn't reject you, you can afford to laugh at misfortunes more easily.

The sun was still pale, and the wind was rather biting, but although Jimmie shivered, the January weather did not seem to trouble his companion who trudged up the hill so fast that Jimmie could hardly keep up with him.

At last they were at the top. Below them they could see the town spread out along the banks of the wide river. Suddenly it became quiet. Too quiet. Jimmie turned to speak to Tom. Tom was not there. He spun round, looking down the side of the hill, but still he could not see him. A thought almost crept into his mind as he called out.

'I'm here,' said Tom. He stood not more than a metre from where he had last been. 'Where did you go?'

Jimmie did not answer. Instead, he suggested that they look for the traces of the Roman fort. They found nothing at all. Eventually they sat down on the grass and looked over the town once more. As they did so, it seemed as if a slight mist passed around them, momentarily, hiding all the surrounding area.

'That's Simmonds'...over there,' said Tom, pointing. Jimmie did not remember having seen the building before. In fact, the whole town looked...wrong. He began to be afraid and he turned to look at Tom, to see if he was still there.

He was. He had not moved, and the expression in his eyes convinced Jimmie that he had nothing to fear from his friend. He even began to doubt the conviction which was growing ever stronger. But then...those clothes, that haircut, that otherness. He thought that Tom understood what he was thinking.

'It's so good to find a *friend* at last,' said Tom.

Jimmie shivered once more. He could not understand why Tom did not wear a sweater, but then...probably he didn't wear one, didn't feel the cold. The strange mist seemed to pass around them once more. The town resumed its customary look. Down on the green, the other boys were still playing. Their cries drifted up on the wind. And what unease had remained left Jimmie. Now he was glad that he had not given way to his fears and run away. That would have been unkind. Obviously Tom needed his help. He must find what it was that kept him here.

'I'll race you to the bottom of the hill,' said Tom.

'Fine,' said Jimmie as he scrambled to his feet. 'But then,' looking at that frail arm, 'what if you fall down?'

'I'll be all right,' replied Tom.

'Of course.' Of course he would be all right. A fall would not hurt *him*.

When they had reached the green once more, Jimmie was almost laughing at himself. Fancy imagining such things! One day he might tell Tom about what he had thought. All those other things he had seen had been tricks of the light, illusions strengthened by the train of his thoughts. The other boys were now coming back towards him, Nick Clark at their head, bouncing Jimmie's ball along the ground as ostentatiously as possible, trying to anger him.

'Where've you been then, Swat-spot?' demanded the bully.

'With a friend,' replied Jimmie.

'What friend?'

When Jimmie turned towards Tom, there was no one there. Perhaps he could see a vague, vague outline of someone, someone desperately trying to cross back into this other world, other time. Nick and his friends only sniggered; they, of course, could not see anything at all, and this was grand fun as far as they were concerned. More ammunition to use against the boy who they already tormented so mercilessly.

'Been seeing ghosts, have you?' jeered Nigel Fleming.

'Yes, actually.' So unexpected was this reply, that the aggressive group immediately drew away from him, looked afraid. If Jimmie were mad, who knew what he would do?

The next day, it was Jimmie's turn to be afraid, and for no reason which he could identify. He was not afraid of Tom now, even if he were a ghost.

Oh yes! He had really accepted that fact now. Tom was a ghost, and, if he could, Jimmie would help him. But he felt that something dreadful was going to happen. He did not want to go to school at all. But he could not persuade his father to let him stay at home. Reluctantly, he opened the front door and stood on the step. When he tried to turn back and run inside, the door was firmly shut. And painted a different colour! Nevertheless, he hammered on it, hoping that whoever were the ghosts in there, they might be friendly and help him back to the world of the living. His pounding fists made no sound. Of course. It was a ghost door.

The town around him now, so unfamiliar except from that brief moment's view from the hilltop, this was a ghost town. The people who passed in the streets were as unaware of him as if he did not exist.

Overhead, a plane passed. For some reason this frightened Jimmie more than anything else in this awful experience. Why?

Now, he wished that he could see at least one familiar face, even Nick Clark. But the pale-visaged inhabitants of this town had obviously been dead long since. They would not know of Nick Clark, nor of Jimmie; *they* were yet to come, yet to be born. And, when it should have been mid-January, it was high summer. For a moment, it seemed that a rag-and-bone man's horse had sensed his presence, lifting its head in his direction and seeming to stare as hard as an animal could. But this was only for the briefest span.

Jimmie screamed. But no sound came. He could not tell whether this was because his throat was paralysed, or because, in this other world, he could not make any physical impression.

Perhaps, if he went back inside the house.... Surely, he would be able to pass through the insubstantial walls. But this was too upsetting an idea for him. What might he find in there? Nothing familiar. Not his father. He ran down the strange street, his feet as soundless as though they were striking on air.

As he came to a corner, he saw a woman in his path, laden with groceries, and he tried to stop, to avoid her. But it was too late. Then he realized that he had passed right through her, and she had been totally unconscious of his presence. He was trapped in a world of ghosts!

He ran on, ran on towards where he guessed he must find the green. Perhaps there he might find some of the other boys whom he knew, from his own time. That was where he had met Tom. Tom! He had forgotten about him in his terror. If he had met the strange boy there, it might be that that was the true crossing place between the two times. If Tom were a ghost, as surely he was, then perhaps he would hold the key to the mystery, would be able to tell him how to reach the Present.

He reached the green, and yes! There was Tom, standing near the edge, where they had first met. Waiting for him. Jimmie had no doubt of that. He ran on towards his ghost friend who looked up, obviously relieved and happy that he had not been abandoned. Then, as the world shifted again, Tom was gone, and the strange town. The school bell was tolling and all the boys who Jimmie knew were hurrying towards it, crossing the playground.

He could not wait now, to find the ghost boy. He must not be late for school. He was only just in time for assembly. Cold and shaking with fear, he took his place in the hall, relieved to be back in the Present, the world of the living. Yet he was pained at having been unable to reach his friend, the only friend he had truly known in years.

Overhead, a plane passed. Nick Clark looked up.

He was standing on the green once more, in that other-time place, with Tom still on the same spot. Both boys looked at one another. They knew for certain now what had been in their minds from the very beginning.

'Come on, Jimmie, I'll show you what it's all about,' said Tom.

'About you being a...ghost?' asked Jimmie.

Tom nodded. In his eyes was the strangest expression of something like sympathy, but even stronger. He beckoned once more, and they crossed the school courtyard which was surrounded by buildings which Jimmie could not recognize.

They stopped in front of one of the unfamiliar buildings, and Tom raised his hand, pointing at a plaque in the wall. He opened his mouth to speak. Jimmie knew now what he was going to say, and started to protest, but the light shifted once more; the world slipped round a little, and he knew.

He was once more in the assembly hall. Nick Clark was still looking up in the direction of the plane, his face fixed in an expression of terror. The bomb struck so quickly that there was no hope of anyone's escaping. Jimmie was lifted off his feet as the flames leapt up round the headmaster's table. Screams tore through the air. Then the second and third bombs fell. And the World went black.

He read the plaque in the wall now:

'ON THIS SITE STOOD THE ORIGINAL BUILDINGS OF THE CAWLEY SCHOOL FOR BOYS, FOUNDED IN 1912, AND DESTROYED BY ENEMY ACTION ON JANUARY 23RD 1941, WITH ALL PUPILS AND MEMBERS OF STAFF.'

'And I thought *you* were the ghost,' said Jimmie. 'But...if I died in Nineteen-Forty-one, what year is this?'

'Nineteen-Seventy-nine,' said Tom.

'And I've been a ghost for thirty-eight years!'

56

Jimmie was so overwhelmed by this, that he could not prevent the tears from welling up. And they burnt on his cheeks! Somehow, he took this as a sign that soon he would be free.

Tom managed to raise his withered arm just enough to touch Jimmie's elbow. 'But you can still be my friend, can't you?'

'Of course I can. That's why I was made to stay here...because I died unhappy, not having anyone to play with.'

A terrible thought struck the other boy. 'But what will happen to you when I'm grown up? I shan't be able to play with you then.'

'By then I'll be free to sleep,' said Jimmie. 'I won't be looking any more. I'll have known what it is to have a friend.'

He smiled as he had not smiled before; and the two boys, revenant and living, ran off in the August sunshine.

THE OWL ON THE LEDGE

by *Genevieve Hawkins*

It was half an hour's walk from the station to the village and Ivor and Barry were glad to sit on the churchyard wall and take off their rucksacks for a moment. Ivor pointed down the lane and across a couple of fields.

'That's the farm. Let's go and report right away.'

They met the farmer before they got there. He waved from his tractor and drove to the edge of the field.

'You the boys who wrote about camping?'

'Yes,' said Ivor. 'I'm Ivor Barlow and this is Barry Heffer. It was very kind of you to agree.'

'No problem. See the castle? You could camp in that field there, won't be in anyone's way. There's a good hedge against the wind. But mind, the castle's not on my land and don't go climbing on the walls, they're not safe.'

'Okay, we won't,' said Ivor. 'Thank you very much.'

'There's a tap in the yard when you want water,' the farmer added, pointing back to the farm buildings. 'We'll see you, I daresay.' He nodded and smiled and the tractor roared away across the field. The boys grinned happily at each other.

'I thought you were going to tell him that your family used to live here,' Barry said as they headed for the castle.

'I did mean to,' said Ivor. 'But it was so long ago, there's no way he could remember them. Tell you what, though, I would like to find my great-grandmother's grave. She always wanted to be buried back here, where she came from.'

'What about your great-grandfather?'

'He was killed in the First World War. She was always talking about him. He came home on leave once, and on his way back his ship was blown up.'

'No medals,' said Barry regretfully.

'No *life*,' said Ivor. 'All he ever wanted was to farm.'

They put up their tent in the shelter of the hedge and collected a pile of sticks but decided not to light a fire until the evening. They sat outside the tent eating pork pies and looking at the castle walls, wishing they could explore them. The one which faced them had a bricked-in Norman doorway and a gaping hole at ground-floor level, and a row of small windows, also bricked-in, much higher up. At a right angle to it, and forward to the left, from the boys' point of view, was a solid stone wall so derelict at the top that it ran in a steep slope, from the upper window level at the back to a height of only about three metres at the front. Wallflowers grew in clumps between the stones.

'Look!' said Barry suddenly. 'There's a white owl on that ledge, below the windows.'

Unmistakeably white, almost brilliantly white, yet nearly twice as big as a barn owl, which was the only white owl that Barry had ever actually seen, it sat on the ledge staring out into space with intent unblinking eyes.

'Ivor! You don't think it could be a *snowy* owl?'

He turned round excitedly, but Ivor was looking out across the fields with an expression on his face that Barry had never seen before, an expression of fierce longing.

'I don't want to go back,' he said hoarsely, 'I don't want to go back.' And his eyes filled with tears.

Barry started to say that they didn't have to go back for three whole days, but felt, as Ivor's face began to twitch, that words were useless. He turned back to look at the owl again, but with interest much diminished for not being able to share it with Ivor. It was there, motionless, on the ledge, and then suddenly, with no movement at all, it disappeared. Barry's mouth fell open and he whipped round to Ivor. Ivor was cheerfully finishing off his pie. He looked inquiringly at Barry. He seemed perfectly carefree.

'What was all that about?' Barry asked, even more amazed by Ivor's changes of mood than by the owl's disappearance.

'All what?'

'When I wanted to show you the owl—'

'What owl?'

'I *told* you—'

'What? I didn't hear you say anything.'

'What have you been thinking about for the last few minutes?'

'My lunch, what else? Did you actually see an owl?'

'Perhaps we'll see it another time,' said Barry lamely, and he ate his bar of chocolate without tasting a single mouthful.

The boys spent a happy afternoon following the course of the river, and came back at dusk very wet and muddy. Barry needed only to change his shoes and socks, which he did outside, while Ivor, who was soaked to the armpits, plunged into the tent to see what other clothes he could muster. Barry got the fire started and shouted to Ivor to bring out the frying pan and the sausages. 'Okay, and the lard!' Ivor shouted back, and at that moment, as he knelt over the fire warming his hands, Barry saw the white owl again. He hadn't seen where it had started from but it was flying, rather floppily, straight towards him and he put up his arm to shield his eyes. It circled round him three times, so close that he could see its great golden eyes, then flew back to the castle and settled on the ledge on which he had first seen it. He could still see its whiteness in the half darkness.

'Ivor,' he called, not too loudly, and he scrambled to the entrance of the tent.

Ivor was crouching at the back of the tent, and when he saw Barry he bared his teeth in something like a snarl.

'I won't go back, I won't go back!' he said, his voice shaking. 'I don't want to die out there in the stinking mud. I don't want to be eaten by filthy rats. I don't want to, I don't want to. I want to live and die and be buried in my own country, alongside of Alice.'

He picked up his boots and hurled them at Barry, hitting him quite hard on the shoulder. Barry sprang backwards and went back to the fire, wondering about trains home the next day. His eyes went to the ledge on the castle wall. The owl was still there, but as he watched it disappeared into thin air.

'Frying pan, sausages, lard,' said Ivor behind him. 'I can't find my boots anywhere, Barry. Hey, what are they doing out here?'

'Don't you know?' said Barry bitterly, but Ivor looked completely blank.

Barry was silent throughout the meal, asking himself the same questions over and over again. Was Ivor mad, and if so, was he dangerous? Or was he just pretending? Both times this had happened just as Barry saw the owl. Was Ivor unnerved by owls? But then the second time Ivor had been inside the tent and couldn't have known that the owl was there. There was nothing for it, he would have to sound him out.

'That white owl came really close to me just now,' he said to Ivor.

'What white owl?'

'The one I saw this morning. I saw it again just now. It flew right round me. I thought perhaps you were scared of it.'

'Thanks a lot. You didn't even tell me it was there.'

'I did. I looked into the tent, and you were gibbering like a halfwit!'

'I was *what*?'

'Sort of gibbering about rats.'

'About *rats*? Why rats?'

'You should know, Ivor,' said Barry angrily. 'You're the one who was on about them.'

'I—don't—understand,' said Ivor through clenched teeth, and he grabbed hold of Barry's sweater and shook it. 'I've never mentioned rats to you, and you've never mentioned owls to me. But you say I have, and you say you have. Are you going mad?'

'No,' said Barry limply, 'no, I thought perhaps you were.'

'Not a chance,' said Ivor, letting go. 'Tell you what, though, I could do with some more to eat. Shall we start on that fruit cake?'

It was impossible to stay angry with Ivor, he was too good-tempered. But it was more than possible to stay frightened, and by the time the boys decided to go to bed Barry had a splitting headache. Ivor dived into his sleeping-bag and fell asleep at once; Barry tossed and turned for an hour, then finally got up, took his torch and went out.

It was not altogether dark; the stars were very bright and there was a three-quarter moon. The gaunt walls of the castle gleamed faintly in the moonlight, the clumps of wallflowers scattered over them casting very black patches of shadow. Barry walked to the bottom of the field and stood looking up at the ledge on which the owl had perched. It ran the full length of the wall, about ten meters up, half a metre or so below the row of windows. In daylight it had looked as if they were all bricked in, but now, with the sharp moonlight shadows, Barry could see quite clearly that the fourth from the left was an open space with an inside wall a very little way behind it, allowing perhaps for a tiny cell or for a passageway. Wishing once again that they had not been asked to keep away from the castle, and feeling now very sleepy, Barry turned and started back towards the tent.

The owl appeared as though from nowhere, flapping, with its talons poised to grab, straight at Barry's face. Barry flung himself to the ground and lay, his heart pounding, his face buried in his arms. When, hearing no sound, he ventured to look up, the owl dropped towards him and skimmed over his head. He waited, keyed up, for the tearing of the claws, but he felt nothing, not even the touch of feathers. He looked up again, and rose to his knees. Instantly the owl was back, making straight for him, its large intent eyes in the smoothly rounded head making it look like a fanatical shaven-headed monk. Again Barry flattened himself on the ground and lay waiting for the assault, his temples pounding and his mouth dry. When at last he dared look up again, the owl was flying back towards the castle. Barry got to his feet. As always when anything happened to him, words and phrases were swirling round and round in his head. 'The worst attack yet.' 'A really bad attack.' And as the word 'attack' made him think of his uncle Sean, who suffered from asthma, it instantly made him think of Ivor. If this had been the worst attack for Ivor too, what pitiful state might he not be in? Barry stumbled towards the tent and crawled inside.

The tent was empty. Ivor's sleeping-bag lay like a discarded skin across his mattress. His clothes and shoes were just as he had left them. His torch was lying by his pillow. But Ivor himself was not there.

What might not Ivor be capable of? In the grip of the unaccountable misery and rage that seemed to come over him, might he not do something drastic? Barry's first thought was the river. It was fast, it was deep, they had found that out this very day when Ivor had lost his foothold in the mud-bank. Would he think of going back there? Barry ran down the field trying to shout. The first few times very little sound came out. Then his voice grew stronger. 'Ivor! Ivor!' he shouted.

Half way over the gate he paused and looked back. As his eyes swept over the castle walls he saw Ivor.

Ivor must have crawled through the barbed wire fence into the next field and climbed up on to the wall from one of the heaps of old stones. He was now working his way along the upward slope of the wall that ran perpendicular to the castle frontage. It was so steep that he was proceeding on all fours, testing the stonework with his hands. His progress was more confident than Barry would have expected: Ivor, he knew, did not care for heights.

The owl was at its usual post on the ledge, motionless as a sentinel. Barry wondered whether it was luring Ivor on, and whether this weird climb was to end in a death leap. Then it occurred to him that the owl had only to disappear for Ivor to be himself again, and that finding himself half way up the castle wall with no idea how he came to be there, he was more than ever likely to fall. He realized at once that he must follow Ivor and be on hand to help if such a thing should come to pass.

By the time Barry had negotiated the fence and the fallen stonework and had started to climb up the wall, Ivor had reached the corner where the two walls met. He stretched out his right arm and gripped the nearest window sill. Then he thrust his right leg out into the emptiness. Eventually, his foot safely found the ledge. His left leg followed. His progress now became much slower. He was standing with his face to the wall on a narrow ledge. All the testing had to be done with his feet. He moved with very small steps, his hands flat against the wall when there was no window sill to grip. It made Barry feel sick to watch him, but he could only give him occasional glances as his own climb needed all his attention. The mortar between the stones was very crumbly and twice a whole stone fell away as he gripped it. When he got to the corner he was gulping for breath. Ivor had reached the fourth window.

Barry was not at all relishing the idea of manoeuvering himself on to the ledge, and he straightened up for a moment to take stock. Ivor was gripping the window sill with his hands. The owl, of which Ivor had taken no notice and which had itself been quite undisturbed by Ivor, was perched on the ledge between the two boys, its white feathers, flecked with brown bars as Barry could now clearly see, glimmering in the moonlight darkness. And then suddenly it disappeared. There was no movement; one moment it was there and the next it was not. And at that same moment Ivor, deserted by whatever energy was driving him, gave a howl of terror.

'It's all right, Ivor, I'm coming!' Barry shouted. 'Stay where you are, I'm coming!' He had clambered on to the ledge almost before he realized it, and was edging along as Ivor had done, concentrating on keeping his balance and on avoiding clutching at wallflower tufts. As he moved he talked, almost mechanically.

'It's O.K., Ivor, stay where you are. Don't move, Ivor, it's all right.' He drew level with him. Ivor was shivering and his teeth were chattering.

'How did I *get* here, Barry? God, I don't *sleepwalk*, do I?'

'Look,' said Barry, 'we can get over this window sill, it's a proper window. Let's try to straddle it. But go easy, we don't know what's on the other side, it may be a sheer drop.' Ivor's eyes widened in fear. Barry tried to sound calm. 'Just one leg over, then we can sit.'

'Sit and think,' said Ivor, trying to be witty, and he hoisted one leg over the sill. Barry did the same.

Between the window and the inside wall that Barry had seen earlier was a spiral staircase. With immense relief the boys climbed through and sat down on the stone steps.

'I vote we wait for daylight before we try to go down,' Barry said. 'It may take us all the way down or it may disintegrate. We shall need a pretty clear view of what we're doing.'

'Look,' said Ivor, still shivering, 'there's a door a few steps up. If we're going to spend the night here we'd be more comfortable on a level floor.'

It was a heavy wooden door with a pattern of ridges. The big iron handle turned. The door creaked open a fraction, and then stuck. The boys pushed and pushed. The ridges proved very uncomfortable to the shoulder.

'We'll have to give up,' Barry gasped at last, and as he spoke the owl flew straight out of the solid wood of the door and wheeled round his head. Ivor, with a look of wild desperation and the strength of a grown man, gave one more push with his shoulder and sent the door flying open. The boys tumbled forward into a small airless room that made them cry out for breath. Ivor, with great determination, pushed the door shut and sat down breathing heavily. Barry, who could see little but the glimmer of the owl's white feathers, pulled his torch from his hip pocket and switched it on.

The owl was perched on the shoulder of what had once been a man and was now, partly covered by tattered khaki rags, a skeleton. It was lying across the floor with its arms outstretched, as a living person lies in sleep. The owl's wide amber eyes were fixed on Barry's face as it moved from the shoulder to the skull and settled on it. As Barry gazed at it, it slowly disappeared, its whiteness fading out down its body and into the skull, which became more and more luminous and began to glow and glimmer in the darkness. Barry turned to Ivor, who was no longer breathing heavily and was staring at the skeleton as hard as Barry.

'The owl—' Barry said. 'It disappeared into the skull. It turned into the skull.'

'I never saw the owl,' said Ivor, 'but the skull...it sort of stands out, doesn't it?' He stared and stared. 'I wonder who he was, and why he was here.'

'The owl wanted us to find him,' said Barry. Then he added: '*He* wanted to be found. I think the owl was him.'

'But I never saw the owl,' Ivor repeated.

'No!' said Barry. 'What happened to you was different. It was as if you turned into someone else.'

'Him?' Ivor suggested, jerking his head at the skeleton. 'Was that how I knew where to come?

But why me? Why me rather than you? And why did he want us to find him?'

They were both silent for a while. Then Barry, who was interested in military history, said tentatively:

'If he was a soldier, he may be wearing an identity disc.' And as Ivor made no protest, he stretched out a thumb and finger and touched the ragged collar. It fell to pieces as he touched it.

'He *is*,' he breathed, feeling suddenly nervous. He shone the torch clumsily on to the metal disc, rubbed it with his thumb, peered closely at it...then jerked backwards, cast a terrified look at Ivor, and retched violently.

'What is it?' Ivor exclaimed. 'What's wrong?' He tried to take the torch from Barry, but Barry struggled with him, saying, 'Don't, don't touch me, keep away!' keeping his face averted all the while. Then he retched again, and Ivor grabbed the torch and shone it down on to the skeleton.

'IVOR BARLOW,' he read aloud.

'It's you, it's you!' Barry cried hysterically. 'Which are you, you or him? How can he be you?'

There was a long silence. When Barry looked fearfully round, Ivor was gazing at the skeleton with an expression of tenderness that made Barry's throat tighten.

'He was my great-grandfather,' Ivor said slowly. 'So he never went back to the front.'

There was another silence. As the truth sank in to Barry's mind he felt ashamed of his panic and found that the horror had passed. He moved closer to Ivor and knelt beside him, gazing down. The fleshless leer of the skull suggested nothing of the face of a real man. But the mind of the man, Barry thought, recalling all the strange

71

words that Ivor had uttered that day, he did know something of.

'We must have him buried with my great-grand-mother,' Ivor said at last.

'Yes,' said Barry with certainty. 'Yes. That was what he wanted.'

THREE GHOSTS

by John Keir Cross

A Story Told The Wrong Way Round

This, as the title suggests, is a ghost story. At least, we *think* it's a ghost story—there seems no other way to explain it all. Or rather, there *is* another way, but somehow it might be more difficult to believe in than ghost themselves are, if you can see what I mean. Either way it's genuine—I can guarantee that; there's no question of the ghosts turning out to be somebody-or-other in disguise (we all hate that kind of story—Michael once went so far as to found one of his famous Leagues against them, side by side with his League Against Twee Fairy Tales and the Anti-Silly-Poems League, which actually got mentioned once in our local paper). No—it's all true. It's all quite clear—except, perhaps (and this is where I really do get frightened—the slightest bit; a kind of eerie shiver all over) except...who *were* the ghosts? I mean...oh, but this is all wrong!—it's the wrong way round completely! It's no way to tell a story and I ought to know better—after all, I did come second in English last year, if that means anything at all.

Well, then: the beginning—so far as we know what the beginning is...

I'm Caroline. I'm the oldest. Next to me is Michael, after him George, then Jennifer, who is only seven and hardly matters (to the story, I mean).

We're not relatives (except for Jennifer, who is Michael's cousin and lives with his family because she's an orphan). We're only friends. We all lived next door to each other in those days—well, under the same roof, really, for Pine Valley House was split up into three separate flats about twenty years before. It was the only house for kilometres, nestling down among the hills, well away from the main road. Michael's father was a painter, mine was a writer and George's was a composer. They looked on themselves as a kind of 'Colony', as I think artistic people call themselves in that kind of arrangement: they were the Pine Valley Group.

Anyway, that's by the way. What really concerns us is what happened in the summer of last year.

We had reached the stage where we were a bit bored with life and each other. It had been raining heavily on and off for almost a whole week, and we had been moping indoors, scowling at books or trying pretty desperately to invent new games. To crown it all, Jennifer decided to have flu, and so she went off to bed and snivelled while Michael's mother made possets and filled up endless hot-water bottles. People went backwards and forwards on tiptoe (you could hear pretty clearly through the old partitions between the flats). If anyone as much as coughed it was a matter of violent whispering from somewhere or other: 'Ssh! Jenny's resting! She has just dozed off—do *please* be careful.'

And of course, all the rest of us were terrified we would get it too. George read in a book that dandelion root juice was a certain safeguard against flu, so he spent hours in his den brewing the strangest-tasting concoction I've ever come across. He made us all swallow it by the litre— then he read in another book that parsley tea was even better and started in on that. George was always reading things in books.

So on and so on, then, till we were at screaming pitch. And then Michael said, quite suddenly late one afternoon when the rain had stopped for half an hour or so, although the sky was still glowering its hardest—he said: 'I'm fed up. If you people want to know what I'm going to do, I'm going up to Firshanger. That's what. And you can please yourselves if you come or not. That's where *I'm* going, anyway.'

George and I looked at him. Firshanger was the old deserted manor about half a kilometre up the hillside that overlooked the house. It was out of bounds—definitely; it was extremely old and no-one had lived in it for years. The floors and ceilings were all unsafe—a tramp had broken his leg the previous spring, falling through one of the landings. That was the reason for its being out of bounds, of course—nothing more sinister than that.

'What are you going to do there?' asked George.

'I don't know. It doesn't really matter. It's just that I'm going. There might be something there to break up this ghastly monotony.'

'We might run into a ghost or two,' I said, trying to be cheerful. 'It looks the very place for them.'

'Ghosts won't tell us to keep quiet, at least,' growled Michael. 'We'll be able to blow our noses without someone yelling at us to make less noise.'

'I wouldn't be too sure about that,' I said, still trying to be cheerful. Then I went to get my coat and George got his. Michael swore that it wasn't going to rain again, and even if it did he didn't mind a bit of wet. And we set off, still pretty gloomy, not in the least inspired by the adventure, and ploughed our way through the fields towards Firshanger.

As it happened, it *was* Michael blowing his nose that seemed to bring the whole thing to a head.

We reached the old manor at the very moment when the rain started again. Great heavy drops came pattering down, filling the air with a sinister whispering as they fell among the leaves and grasses. Far off there was a rumbling of thunder, and a brisk gust of wind caused a window to shut with a slam.

'Well, there's no going back now, anyway,' said George. 'We'll have to shelter inside while the rain lasts.'

Getting inside presented no difficulties. We found the window that had slammed in the wind—a small lattice round the corner with half the lozenges cracked or missing altogether and the rusty latch fallen onto the sill. There was an immense clump of stinging nettles directly under-neath, but George took his mac off and laid it down on them, so that we were able to climb up without any damage to our bare legs: Michael first, then myself, then George bringing up the rear and pulling his mac up after him like the last de-fender of a castle hauling in the drawbridge. There was another peal of thunder—much nearer this time—and the heavy raindrops in an instant grew into a lashing downpour, driving against the few remaining panes with a ferocious sharp crackle.

'Enemy guns,' grunted George. 'Heavy artillery backing up a machine-gun attack...'

We looked round, rather more interested in things now that the expedition was under way. Before us stretched a long low corridor, the walls all cracked and peeling, great patches of lathing bare in the ceiling where the plaster had fallen. The floor was blanketed thickly in dust, the few boards that were showing seemed worm-eaten and crumbly.

'Go carefully,' said Michael. 'Keep close to the wall—the boards'll be stronger there. Try every step.'

We crept gingerly forward, crouching low and feeling our way in the gloomy light. We came to the first door and pushed it open. A low creak and a long eerie sigh went echoing all round us as the hinges groaned and the door brushed over the sill.

'Nothing there,' said George. 'Phew! This dust!—it's making my eyes smart. Any ghosts in this place are welcome to it as far as I'm concerned.'

By this time we had reached the main hallway. A great curving flight of steps, festooned with cobwebs, ran up from it to the second floor. A small bright-eyed mouse was sitting quite calmly on the balustrade. It stared at us for a moment and we stared back; then it darted down a banister at an incredible speed and disappeared into a hole in one of the steps with a tiny flurry of dust.

We laughed and moved forward again.

'Not the stairway,' said Michael. 'It looks too far gone—we'll stay on the ground floor for the moment—there may be another stairway round the back that will be safer.'

In the great hallway his voice went echoing weirdly.

'...safer,' we heard, quite clearly from upstairs.

'What's that?' gasped George. And——

'...that?' came the voice from the landing.

'It's either an echo or those ghosts of mine,' I said, smiling. And the echo went:

'...osts of mine.'

We were delighted, and carried out some experiments as to which position in the hallway was the best for echo purposes. From outside, as we explored, came the steady swish-swish of the downpour in the trees and against the windows. There was a strange oppressiveness in the atmosphere—the air felt hot and heavy. All round us the ancient house seemed to loom with a kind of silent menace—it was impossible not to feel slightly eerie. I could not help glancing a little apprehensively up the stairway and along the dusky upper landing to reassure myself that there really *was* nothing there—that there was no quiet figure lingering in the shadows and regarding us.

'That looks an interesting room,' said George. 'Let's try that one.'

He was pointing to a massive black-painted

doorway close to the foot of the stairs. We moved across to it, still stepping carefully, and George put his hand out to the handle. He began to turn it.

'Wait a moment,' said Michael. 'This confounded dust...I want to blow my nose.'

He took out his hanky—and blew. And, on that instant, everything seemed to happen at once. From directly overhead, as if it had taken the nose blowing as its cue, there came a sudden ferocious clap of thunder—a great startling peal that made the whole house tremble. Clouds of dust puffed up from the stairway as it quivered in the impact. A blob of plaster fell from the upper ceiling, spraying over the banisters beside us and spurting out on the floor at our feet in a jagged white blot.

'Coo!' said Michael facetiously. 'I never knew I was all that strong?'

I would have laughed—it would have been a kind of relief from the tension I was feeling (for the thunder had been close and I've always been nervous of it). But I had no time to laugh, for George had given a long low whistle and was gripping my arm. Besides, I had seen for myself....

At the moment of the thunder-clap George had pushed the big door open. All three of us had— involuntarily, I suppose—taken a step forward into the room.

And it was such a room!—no room to find in an ancient, deserted manor house—no room to step into without warning, to be confronted with at a moment like that! Yet, strange as it was, it was not the room itself that caused us to freeze there in utter dismay, with shivers going up and down our spines and the little hairs tingling.

In the room, standing facing us, quite calm and

quiet, and yet themselves with a startled air, as if they were as surprised as we were, were three children—two girls and a boy. And we knew, even in that first moment as we looked at them, that they were not from our world—were not any part of it at all…

Well, there it is: that's the first climax—or rather it's the only climax, for I want to emphasise that this is not really a story at all—there is no complex plot, piling incident upon incident and ending in a spectacular burst of excitement. It is only the account of an occurrence—of something strange that happened once, for which there never has been any real explanation, no matter how much we have pondered. An incident—no more than that: an afternoon in late summer, an ancient house high up on a hillside, two boys and a girl on an exploring expedition—and, confronting then suddenly, quite simply and obviously from another world altogether, two girls and a boy.... Three ghosts.

For a long time, as we stood there in the doorway, with the Others facing us across the room, there was an absolute silence and stillness—not one of us moved or spoke. We were frozen like waxworks, George a little ahead of Michael and me, his hand on my arm, his mouth pursed up from the whistle he had given: and the Other Three equally statuesque, the boy in the middle, one of the girls slightly stooped, as if she had been in the act of picking something up.

It was she—the stooping girl—who broke the tension. She straightened herself quite suddenly and smiled—and it was the smile, I think, that dispelled my last lingering tremors of slight fear. It was so pleasant and confident, so completely frank and happy.

'Good afternoon,' she said, in a sweet clear voice, just the smallest bit nasal in intonation. 'You are very welcome. You frightened us for a moment at first, but we can see that you will not harm us. We are very pleased that you came...'

She spoke—as they all did, we discovered—very carefully, pronouncing each syllable distinctly. Her accent was strange on our ears—a gentle lilting sing-song. The shape of some of the words she used was quite different from what we were accustomed to—she said, for instance, *af*ternoon and wel*come*.

'Not at all,' said Michael vaguely. 'I mean—well... How-d'you-do...'

All three bowed gravely at that and said 'how-do-you-do' in their turn. Then there was a moment while we all stared again, not knowing what to say or do next. And during it I surveyed the Three more closely and glanced round the curious room.

The most impressive thing about the Three was their dress. They wore loose tunics of some fine silky material, beautifully cut and apparently all of one piece, so that it seemed to mould itself and flow perfectly with their movements. The colours were soft and harmonious. The girls' costumes were skirted, the boy's was a kind of shirt-and-trousers affair in one—a sort of bib-and-brace overall, exquisitely made. His hair was close cropped. The girls wore their hair in a most unusual style, quite unlike anything I have ever seen—swept up on one side and falling loose on the other; it was altogether most attractive and effective.

Yet it was not so much the appearance of the Three that impressed and intrigued us. There was, all about them, a strange and alien look—a *feeling* that they were quite different from us.

As for the room—how can I begin to describe it? Everything in it was strange and unusual. We recognised a table—but it was not like any table we knew; it was long and low and made of some completely transparent material that seemed to glow internally with a soft greenish light. The chairs were infinitely comfortable in appearance, huge shapely pouffes, as it were, all gentle curves. The floor was covered with a kind of yielding rubbery substance, also of a pale-green colour. On the walls, which were smooth, and covered, as it seemed, with a layer of the same transparent glowing material as the table was made of, were several pictures—photographs; and they, perhaps, were the strangest of all, for not only were the colours brighter and more natural than in any coloured photographs I know, but the subjects seemed to stand out—were completely stereoscopic (George tells me that's the proper word—and assures me that you will know what it means). Two of the photographs were portraits—of a man and a woman; and in both there was a striking resemblance to the Three who faced us. To crown all, the backgrounds to the pictures seemed to be in a kind of constant movement—behind the woman's face, for instance, which stood out quite startlingly and realistically, there was a river scene; and it was as if the river were continually flowing, while the trees on its banks swayed gently to and fro as if in the softest of breezes.

All round this curious room, on shelves and smaller tables, were what I took to be toys—it was as if the room were a playroom or nursery. But what toys! I wish I could describe them—I wish I even had time to mention them all! Model aeroplanes of exquisite, streamlined design, made of the glowing material; other models that seemed to be of motor-cars of a kind—long, low, powerful-looking machines, the originals of which must have been of astonishing speeds; instruments of various sorts (George swears there was a 'super-super-microscope' among them)...a host of things, most of them recognisable, but all strangely different from anything that we ourselves knew.

And all the time while we were surveying them the Three were surveying us. They looked at us closely, smiling all the while. And I wondered if, to them, our outlines were as indistinct and wavery as after a moment or two theirs seemed to us...for it was as if, as we stood there, a queer vibration was in the air, a kind of trembling and quivering in the atmosphere itself—the strange unsteadiness you sometimes notice on a very hot day. The whole room trembled so—the table, the chairs, the very walls...the image of all we saw was imperfect and insubstantial.

I wish we'd had time—I *wish* we'd had more time! I mean, if George is right, if the explanation is what he says it is...what might we not have done, what might we not have found out? But we didn't realise, you see—and the whole thing was over so quickly, almost before we had time to realise what was happening. And besides, when the shock came—when we actually saw...what else could we do but act as we did?

Well, the wrong way round again: I never seem to learn!

It was the boy who broke the second silence. He advanced a little towards us and said, in the same thin, sing-song accents as the girl had used:

'May we introduce? My name is Kannet; this—' pointing to the taller girl—the one who had spoken, '—is Kala; and this is Gem. Come closer a little and tell us your own names. Do not worry, please—we are not afraid.'

Feeling faintly sheepish we moved forward towards the table. George made an awkward gesture and announced our names. I can confess I felt myself blushing—there's something perfectly horrid in one's name when you hear it said out loud and everyone is waiting to know what it is. I looked nervously down at the translucent surface of the table and fingered a little booklet that was lying on it.

'Tell us how you got here,' went on Kannet. 'Weselves arrived only yesterday for our hoddays—we came by robocopter. Was this your house before once?—parents said it was an old house and perhaps it might be peopled—you know, in that way.'

(This whole speech was puzzling—they had a queer manner of putting words together—and the words themselves had an unusual flavour: 'weselves'—and 'parents' where we would have said 'Mother and Father'—and 'hoddays', which confused us a little at first, but which we decided could only have meant holidays.)

'Oh no,' said Michael. 'We only came to...well, have a look round, you know. We don't really live here. Our house is further down the valley. Pine Valley House, you know,' he added.

Immediately the Three exchanged glances. And Gem (she was smaller and prettier than Kala) burst out quickly:

'Pine Valley! Oh! Then you *are*...'

She hesitated, and there was the faintest flicker of fright in her eyes.

'I mean,' she went on, '—you must be very old!'

'Have a heart!' said George. 'I'm fourteen, you know—Mike's thirteen past in June, and Carrie's fifteen a week tomorrow.'

Kala smiled.

'I think Gem meant because of the house,' she said. 'Your house. It has always been called The Ruins by everyone in the district here.'

'The Ruins!' cried Michael. 'You must be making a mistake—we've only just come from there!'

'But it *is* The Ruins,' said little Gem. 'Pine Valley

House. I remember—parents told us. It was burnt down almost exactly a hundred years ago.'

We looked at her in amazement. Then George laughed. It was extraordinary the way our conversation was developing—it was the last thing that any of us would have imagined: arguing calmly with ghosts and them telling us lies in a kind of simple, earnest way that was very puzzling.

'I don't know who you are,' said George grandly. 'You're the biggest surprise I've ever come across in my life. Mind you, I like the look of you, and we're not in the least bit frightened, the way people are supposed to be in situations like this. If we can be friends, that's O.K.—but let's get things quite straight at the outset. Pine Valley House is as little of a ruin as I am myself! And if you doubt my word, have a look! There—you can see it down in the valley.'

He strode across to the window with a magnificent gesture. Michael and I crowded after him. For a moment we stayed quite still, and then a real wave of horror swept through us—the amazement after the thunderclap was nothing compared to it.

Below us, bright in the sunshine, lay the great expanse of the valley. There was no trace of rain— the sky was brilliant and blue. Instead of the tumbling wilderness that we had seen as the garden of Firshanger was a trim, neat lawn, bordered by well-kept flower-beds. Beyond, stretching over the green hills, were rows and rows of houses where before there had been nothing at all—strange, flat little houses of unusual design, but undoubtedly houses.

Yet although we saw and registered these things, what engaged us most was Pine Valley

House. There it lay, far beneath us, clear in the sparkling sunshine. But it was not Pine Valley House as we had known it...It was no more indeed than a crumbling heap of blackened ruins.

I think I screamed—George seems to remember that I did. But it was Michael who acted. He gave a great yell and started to run—and George and I followed him. We ran past the Three and across the yielding rubber carpet. We reached the door, which was still ajar. We tumbled through it and George, bringing up the rear, gave it an enormous slam.

For a second there was an intensification of the quivering in the air, and then we were in the hallway of Firshanger—the ancient dusty hallway.

Michael tugged at the great front door. A gust of rain swept into our faces. We ran—down the hill and through the fields like mad things. We reached Pine Valley, our hearts in our mouths.

The house stood fair and square to our gaze, no trace of burning or ruin about it.

Bewildered we rushed inside. Michael's mother met us.

'Children, children,' she cried. 'Do be *quiet*! I've told you a hundred times if I've told you once. Jenny's resting—she's just dozed off...'

Well, well! What would *you* have made of it?

You would have done the same as we did. You would have gone back up the hill to Firshanger, rain or no rain. You would have gone through the front door. With only a momentary hesitation you would have opened the other door—the black one beside the stairway.

And you would have found what we found. A mouldering, ancient room, quite empty, smothered in dust...

We puzzled over the whole thing for three days—we thought about nothing else, we talked about nothing else. The weather cleared, the sun shone brilliantly—the very thing we had longed for for more than a week. But it made no difference; we still sat and moped indoors, glooming at our parents when they tried to persuade us to go outside, avoiding Jenny, who was convalescing, as if she were the plague.

At the end of three days three things happened. I shall finish my story calmly and quite without any comment by putting them down in the proper order. (I wish I never *had* been second in English!—either I do the wrong thing altogether in story-telling or, if I do the right thing, I do it in quite the wrong place!)

The first thing was that George came over to where Michael and I were sitting in the window seat gazing hopelessly across the valley towards Firshanger.

'I've been reading a book,' said George profoundly.

We scowled at him: George was always reading books.

'It was a book about Time,' went on George. 'A scientific book about travelling in Time..."

'So what?' growled Michael. 'Even if it were possible, what's it got to do with anything?'

'Only that I believe we may have done it,' George said mildly. 'Travelled in Time, I mean...'

We looked at him sharply, but he seemed quite sane and balanced. He sat down between us.

'Look here, you two,' he said, and his voice was very grave and serious. 'I believe I may have solved it. I may be wrong, of course, but it's the only thing that fits in. I won't go into detail—I can't, it's far too technical. But it boils down to this, in a nutshell: people *move* in Time—it's yesterday, then it's today, and then it's tomorrow. Time flows, like a river—it goes on. It has a *course*. Now, for a long while scientists have been thinking about the possibility of actually travelling in Time—of going into the past or into the future at will. You've both read H. G. Wells' story of *The Time Machine*. Well, then: I believe that when we three were standing by that doorway in Firshanger three days ago, a curious thing happened—there was an accident in Time. I believe that that thunder-clap did something—did something quite extraordinary. You remember the vibration from it?—the tremendous impact it made on the house? I believe that that impact *pushed* us—in some freakish way it pushed us right out of the present altogether. It pushed us forward—we slipped suddenly across years and years and years...into the future. We were *there*, rather precariously—remember the wavering in the air?—in a different Time altogether. And when I slammed the door behind us as we ran out of he room, we slipped again beneath *that* impact—back into the present.'

'The future?' I asked in bewilderment. And George nodded gravely.

'The future. Kala and Kannet and Gem were people of the future—real people. When we looked out of the window we saw a landscape of the future—a real landscape. Somewhere between now and then, whenever it was, a new house was built—I should say *will* be built—on the site of Firshanger. And we were in it—that day we were in it!'

There was an impressive silence.

'Then they weren't three ghosts,' said Michael softly. 'If you're right, that is.'

'No—they weren't...But there *were* Three Ghosts at Firshanger that day all the same. Consider—if they were out of the future to us, we were out of the past to them. And ghosts are said to be creatures out of the past. There *were* Three Ghosts, my friends—and they were us!'

Well, that was the first thing. The second was a little more spectacular. It grew directly out of the first thing, for George said, after a little while when we had talked things over for a bit:

'Ah! If only we had brought something back with us—if *only* we had!'

And in an instant I remembered. I remembered my embarrassment at the moment when we were being introduced to Kala and the others. I remembered the little book on the table that I had been fingering—and I remembered that I still had it in my hand while we were staring out of the window.

I jumped up and ran for my mac. I fumbled in the pockets and in an instant I was back with the others and we were poring over it excitedly.

It was a diary—it was Gem's diary; her name was written in it in a precise angular script: *Gemma Peacock*. It was made of some smooth plastic substance that was very but not quite like paper.

We thumbed it through quickly. There were entries up to the 3rd August, blank pages from there to the end.

'The 3rd August,' breathed George. 'And the year—A.D. 2082.... A hundred years exactly!'

He was pointing to the top of the page, where the date was clearly printed in small, unusually formed characters.

'Gem said something herself about "a hundred years exactly",' I murmured, half to myself. And then I remembered what she *had* said—and sprang up in dismay. 'Good heavens,' I cried. 'Then that means...'

And the third thing happened. And it was the most spectacular of all. And it answered my thoughts—it finished my sentence.

There was a sudden cry from Michael's mother. 'Fire! Fire!' And a startled scream, and a rushing of feet...

It seemed, you see, that Rover, Michael's half-blind old dog, had knocked over one of the little oil-stoves Michael's mother used for cooking. The ancient house went up like tinder—there was no hope for it. It was impossible to get help quickly enough from the town—Pine Valley was too inaccessible.

We were all saved—we even managed to retrieve most of our belongings. But the house itself was doomed. Within six hours we were all standing disconsolately on the hillside looking down at a heap of blackened ruins. Michael and George and I could hardly tell the others that we had seen them before—overgrown with weeds and rather more decayed and crumbled, but essentially the same: only... a hundred years older.

The Ruins—as they were to be called from that day on. And somewhere among them, alas, forgotten in all the turmoil and excitement—burnt completely to ashes, I expect—was Gem's little diary.

Well, that was a year ago. It's the story of the Three Ghosts at Firshanger—written down by one of them.

MISTY

by Margaret Biggs

Paddy sat on the windowsill, her legs warmed by the radiator, and looked wistfully across the road at the Peytons' white-painted house, where the bulky removal van stood. It was a rough, windy day, and the men's hair whirled over their faces as they carried the Peytons' desk down the garden path.

'I *do* wish they weren't going,' thought Paddy, from her heart.

The Peytons were going to Yorkshire. Mrs Peyton was kind, lively and friendly, and, to painfully shy Paddy, an unexpectedly easy person to talk to. Mrs Peyton really listened—rare, in Paddy's experience. But the big attraction to Paddy, and the main cause of her sadness, was Misty, Mrs Peyton's undersized smoky-grey cat. How she would miss Misty!

Paddy was an only child, and she had always passionately wanted a cat. But her mother, over-protective and inclined to fuss, refused, alarmed at the possible germs and general upheaval a cat would bring into the household.

'No, Paddy, we can't possibly have a cat. You know your father's allergic to them. And I'm sure you'd catch something—heaven knows, you miss enough school as it is, with all your coughs and colds. No, I've made up my mind, and you'll just have to make the best of it. We're not having a cat, so don't keep on about it.'

After several years of arguing and beseeching, Paddy by now had reluctantly come to realize that there was no shifting her mother; so she did the next best thing, and made a fuss of any cats who lived near. Misty—beguiling, soft, emerald-eyed, purring deafeningly when a certain spot under her chin was tickled, was her favourite. She was, in fact, Paddy's best friend. Paddy turned to animals rather than girls of her own age, who didn't seem to think along her lines. At school she was always a loner, never part of a gang. She felt the others regarded her critically, and so stayed silent. But when she walked slowly home along the quiet road, Misty, unapproachable to most people, would appear as if by magic, and rub against her legs, rolling over in ecstasy when Paddy stooped down and lovingly stroked her.

Misty haunted Paddy's garden, and sat in the apple tree or slept under the redcurrant bushes.

Sometimes she even prowled up and down outside Paddy's bedroom window, having jumped lightly up from the garage roof. Paddy would look up from chewing a pencil over her homework and see Misty gazing unblinkingly at her through the glass. She would go to the window and carry Misty inside for a while, ready to pop her quickly out if she heard her mother coming upstairs. With Misty on her lap, homework went with a swing. Misty's drowsy purr seemed to clear Paddy's head, and helped solve all problems more quickly.

Two months before, Misty had had kittens. That had been thrilling. Mrs Peyton had excitedly called Paddy across to see the basketful of mewing, squirming little blind soft-haired kittens, with Misty lying protectingly, watchfully beside them.

'Oh, aren't they sweet! Oh, I do wish I could have one!' And Paddy knelt down and stroked them gently, and then fondled Misty, telling her how clever she was, while Misty arched her neck in proud agreement.

Mrs Peyton looked sympathetically down at the girl. Much too thin, she thought, and waif-like, with big, serious, grey eyes and dark hair falling untidily around her pale face.

'I suppose your mother wouldn't let you have one, Paddy, when they're bigger? We shall have to find good homes for them—though I'd love to keep them all, they're so heavenly!'

'You know I'd simply love one—specially this little grey one, just like Misty. He's even got the same tiny stripes on his chin, hasn't he? But Mum won't let me.' Paddy sighed, then met Mrs Peyton's eye and added, in defence of her mother: 'She doesn't mean to be unkind, you know. She gets so worked up when I'm ill, that's the trouble, and she's got a thing about animals and their germs.'

'Well, we have to live in the same world as germs, so I try not to dwell on them. But I know your mother does it for the best, dear,' said Mrs Peyton. She did indeed, for she liked Mrs Bailey, always a kind neighbour, despite being a born worrier. 'Anyhow, you come over and visit them as much as you like, won't you? Misty loves to see you—in fact, she's as much your cat as mine, isn't she?'

Paddy's pale face glowed at this comforting idea. 'I never thought of it like that. Thanks, Mrs Peyton.'

The kittens grew up into enchanting, naughty little fighters, rolling over and perpetually biting at each other. As they grew older and rougher, Misty sometimes became angry when they continually disturbed her by pouncing at her tail or pulling her whiskers, and she would cuff them and stalk off, tail twitching indignantly.

'They'll probably be her last litter. She's twelve now, and that's elderly for a cat,' said Mrs Peyton. 'She finds them a bit too much of a good thing. She'll be glad when they're grown up and she can get some peace.'

'I didn't know she's the same age as me,' said Paddy. She hesitated, watching two kittens trying with all their might to catch their tails. 'Have— have you found homes for any of them yet, Mrs Peyton?'

'Yes. I put a card in the newsagent's window, and several people have phoned. I shall miss them, but they're quite a handful. And besides——' Mrs Peyton hesitated, then took the plunge. 'We've got to move, Paddy. My husband's firm are sending us up to Yorkshire. We only heard yesterday.'

As she had expected, Paddy was upset and appalled. Her grey eyes widened in horror. 'Oh, Mrs Peyton, that's awful—gosh, I shall miss you terribly—and Misty. Oh, my darling Misty!' She went over and picked up Misty, hugging her tightly, in a fashion that would have called up her mother's horrified remonstrances.

'I'm terribly sorry myself. We don't want to go a bit, but we haven't any choice.' Mrs Peyton sighed. Touched by Paddy's stricken face, she went on: 'I tell you what—you must come and stay with us in the summer holidays. Will you? We'll fix a definite date.'

Paddy nodded. She knew Mrs Peyton meant it, and it would be *something*, but the summer holidays were months away. She went home very glum. And over the next few weeks, though she tried to hide it, she remained sad. She watched enviously as various people called at the house opposite and collected the kittens. One by one they went, eager and independent now, until by moving day there was only one left, the little grey and white tom, smaller and quieter than the rest. 'Misty's favourite, he is,' said Mrs Peyton, watching the kitten trot solemnly after his mother across the kitchen floor. 'I must admit I'm glad he's left. We'll take him with us—he'll be company for his mum. He doesn't tease her like the others.'

She didn't say it, but she deeply wished Paddy could keep the kitten. In fact, she even dared to suggest it to Paddy's mother, the day before they moved.

'He's a dear little well-behaved animal. I'm sure you wouldn't find him any trouble, and he's house-trained.'

But Mrs Bailey shook her head decisively. 'It's

97

nice of you to offer, and I feel mean about it, but I've never felt happy with cats. They make my husband sneeze, you know. And then there'd be all the hairs on the furniture. But the main thing is Paddy's health. She's delicate, you know.'

Mrs Peyton longed to argue, wishing she could make Mrs Bailey change her mind. What did a few hairs matter? she thought, as she returned to her always untidy house. People were more important than the houses they lived in. But Mrs Bailey really *did* believe she was doing the right thing, so what was the good of trying to alter her?

Now the day of the Peytons' move had inexorably arrived, and the men were loading up the last of the furniture. Paddy was still watching, absently chewing a strand of her hair, when she saw Mrs Peyton scurrying about the front garden, cat-box in hand, looking unusually distraught, with her coat on, ready to go, and her hair blowing about in the cold wind. Her husband had a word with the men, and then looked anxiously up and down the road. Now the van was moving lumberingly off, and Mrs Peyton was coming hurrying across. Paddy jumped up and ran out to meet her.

'Oh, Paddy, I can't find Misty and the kitten anywhere. I shut them in the shed to keep them safe, but one of the men went to get the mower out, and they were frightened and ran off. We've looked everywhere. I'm so worried, and my husband says we've got to be going. Will you help me look? Misty might come out if she heard your voice. You're her favourite.'

'I'll come—I'll just grab my anorak,' Paddy said, and flew back into the house. Her mother would never forgive her if she went without it on a cold day like this.

She and Mrs Peyton called till they were hoarse, and searched the empty house energetically, all the echoing rooms and cupboards, the garage— even peering along the dusty shelves—and, just to be sure, the shed once more. But there was no sign of the two small animals, and Mr Peyton prowled about, increasingly impatient.

Paddy raced around the garden, where the trees bent painfully in the strong wind, and then charged back into her own and craned up at the apple tree, which creaked noisily, and beneath the redcurrant bushes. But no use, and now Mr Peyton was calling impatiently: 'We promised to give the keys to the agent by half past twelve, and it's past that already. I know you're upset, love——' as his wife gazed despairingly at him—'but honestly we've just *got* to go. Look, Paddy will keep her eyes open and ring us at the new house, won't you, Paddy? As soon as they're spotted, we'll drive back somehow, though it's inconvenient, heaven knows, and I've got a million more important things to do.'

'Well——' said his wife slowly, for once not knowing what to say.

'If we don't get a move on, we won't get there in time to let the men in with the furniture at the new house. Keep a sense of proportion, love, for goodness' sake!'

Mrs Peyton had to give in. The last sight Paddy saw was her worried face forcing an unconvincing smile as she got into the car, and her heartfelt: 'Paddy, I know I can rely on you—if they come across to you later, ring straight away, won't you? I do hate going off like this, but I've got to. If only I'd put them in the cat-box earlier—but Misty hates it, so I thought I'd wait: Oh, all right, Bill,

I'm coming, aren't I?'

Mr Peyton switched on the engine and smiled briefly at Paddy. 'Good girl—you've written our phone number down, haven't you? We simply must dash now. See you soon!' And the car, loaded with cardboard boxes and carrier-bags stuffed full of oddments, roared off down the quiet road, with Mrs Peyton waving frantically.

'Don't worry, I'll look out for them. They can't be far away,' Paddy shouted. She was as upset as Mrs Peyton.

She turned then, aware of her mother standing beside her, waving. Her mother said briskly: 'It's just as I always say. Pets are such a nuisance—as if there aren't enough problems!'

'Oh, Mum, how can you? They're no more a nuisance than people!' flared Paddy.

And Mrs Bailey, affronted and about to make a tart response, saw the distress in her daughter's eyes and said more gently: 'Well, I expect they'll turn up when they're hungry. Don't get so worried. It isn't *your* problem, remember.' Which was funny, Paddy thought, coming from her mother, who never stopped worrying…

Over the next few days, Paddy, having tramped around the Peytons' empty garden once more, gave up there and concentrated on asking all the other neighbours if she could look in their gardens as well. She pestered everyone in the road, in fact, and neglected everything else. Where *could* Misty and her kitten have got to? Paddy lay awake each night worrying, and went into a trance at school thinking about them. Twice she got told off for not listening. They must have wandered off and might be anywhere now, lost, miserable and hungry. That was unbearable.

Strange, too, she thought. Misty had never been a cat for wandering far. She had always stayed close to base, a real home-lover. So she *must* be somewhere near, if only Paddy could find her. And then thoughts of car accidents haunted her.

Mrs Peyton rang up two days after the move, and sounded distraught.

Paddy told her all she was doing.

'You're a dear, Paddy. I'm so grateful! If they turn up here I'll let you know. Cats do sometimes find their way over incredible distances, don't they?' floated Mrs Peyton's hopeful voice, all the way from Yorkshire.

'I don't really see how they could,' said Paddy regretfully. 'It's two hundred kilometres, isn't it?' Geography wasn't her strong point. 'After all, Misty's kitten isn't very big.'

'I know.' Mrs Peyton's sigh travelled over the wire. 'Oh, Paddy, if *only* we hadn't had to move. I can't settle to anything here for worrying. Well, I'm sure Misty would come to you, if to anybody. I won't give up hope.'

Nor would Paddy. Despite her mother's protests, and her father's doubtful expression, she went on hoping—and looking.

One morning, ten days after the Peytons had moved, Paddy woke up with a great start. It was still very early—a grey, filmy light glimmered through the curtains, and one or two of the first birds were starting drowsily to sing. Was that what had woken her? Paddy lay warm and comfortable, sleepily listening. And then, unbelievably, she heard a faint, persistent mewing. She sat up, startled, and saw a grey, familiar shape pressed against the window, in the gap between the curtains. It was Misty, it must be, back on her old

perch! Her heart pounding, Paddy jumped out of bed.

'Misty, Misty—are you here after all?' she whispered delightedly. As she crossed the room she saw Misty's frantic, grey-furred face, her open mouth, her beseeching look. Then, as Paddy reached the window, to her astonishment she saw there was nothing there. No small cat clung to the narrow window-ledge.

Bewildered, Paddy opened the window and craned out, regardless of the chill morning air blowing across her hair and face. There was nothing, whichever way she looked. Below lay the silent, empty garden, and the apple tree looming in the grey morning light. But there was no movement, and no sound save the chirping of the wakening birds. Paddy stood still, shivering, motionless, unable to understand.

'It *was* Misty,' she told herself. 'And she wanted me to help her, terribly. But where is she?'

She mentioned the inexplicable incident to nobody. She was afraid of being laughed at—and her mother might even have kept her in bed a day, saying she was over-tired, which was a favourite expression of hers. Before she went off to school, Paddy searched her own garden, just in case—but, of course, as she expected, she found nothing.

She picked at her food that night, and aroused her mother's immediate anxiety. 'Oh, Paddy, surely you're going to eat more than that! You look pale. Are you sickening for something?'

'No, Mum. I'm just not hungry.'

Mrs Bailey eyed her only child closely. 'Well, do have a glass of milk,' she said coaxingly.

'No, thanks, Mum. I'll have some later. I ought

103

to get on with my homework.'

Her father said quietly, when Paddy had escaped to her bedroom: 'Don't fret so over her. She'll eat when she's hungry. No need to make a great production over it.'

'But she's hardly had a thing! Oh, Ray, d'you think I should go and take her temperature?' Mrs Bailey half rose.

'*No.*' Mr. Bailey sounded unusually firm. 'Leave her alone. It's this lost cat she's worrying about.'

'I do wish she'd forget all that nonsense. Such a wretched thing to happen, but just like Mrs Peyton. She always was inclined to be careless.' Mrs Bailey sighed. 'If only Paddy wouldn't moon round animals so much!'

'Hmm,' said Mr Bailey. He liked animals himself, but he liked a quiet life even more, and for this reason had given in to his nervy wife about not keeping pets. But lately he was beginning to wonder if he had done the right thing. If Paddy was really unhappy, perhaps he should open up and say what he thought, for once.

Paddy managed with difficulty to drink a large mug of cocoa that her mother brought up to her, while she was doggedly doing her homework, but later, when she went to bed, she couldn't sleep. She heard her parents come up, and kept her eyes tight shut and her breathing regular when her mother, as she always did, anxiously peeped in on her. Soon the house was silent, but she was still wide awake. 'Oh, Misty, where *are* you?' she said aloud. She was deeply convinced that the two cats were somewhere near, desperately trying to reach her. The feeling had grown on her urgently all day.

Just as at last, after what seemed ages, she was

drifting off into a light, uneasy sleep, the sound of scrabbling claws woke her with a jerk. Again came that faint, frantic mewing, weaker now, but still determined.

She must be at the window again, thought Paddy, her stomach lurching. Oh, if only I could understand...

Without putting the light on, she stumbled in the darkness to the window. She pushed back the curtains. For a second she saw a dark blur. She flung open the window and felt a touch of soft fur brush against her cheek. 'Misty!' she cried, putting out her hands. But they touched only the air. She clicked on the light. As she had expected, there was nothing there.

The next day was wet and wild. The wind raged and roared through the branches of the apple tree. It was a Saturday, so there was no school. After breakfast, having forced down a boiled egg under her mother's vigilant gaze, Paddy zipped herself up into her red anorak and went out across the road and into the Peytons' familiar empty garden.

This will be the last time, she thought stoically. The new people are coming in on Monday, and I shan't be able to look any more. It won't be any good, of course, because I've looked everywhere over and over again. But this will be the last time, and then I can't do any more, and I'll never understand...

Systematically she ploughed through the dripping branches of the Peytons' trees. Rain splashed into her face. A wet branch dug her neck, and made her jump. A last time she peered through the shed window, but through the rain streaming down the glass she could see it was bare and completely empty. For once she walked on right to where Mr Peyton used to burn his weeds at irregular intervals. She had not gone so far before, only glanced that way. There was nothing, of course, but the pile of wet leaves—and, beyond, a wooden crate, iron-banded, up-ended. Mr Peyton used to chop up crates for wood to light the boiler. Paddy stood in the drizzling rain, looking rather hopelessly at the rubbish heap. Suddenly she rushed over to the crate, ignored hitherto, and pushed it sideways. Her heart was banging suddenly, like a live creature leaping inside her. The crate was surprisingly heavy, but yielded at last to her pushing and fell reluctantly sideways. Inside it she knew what she could find, and was poignantly right. Two still small bodies lay there, Misty and the kitten, crouched together asleep—or dead? Paddy knelt down in the mud, gently touching them.

'Misty, oh Misty, were you caught in here all the time? Oh, *why* didn't I see? I never thought...'

Misty's small, thin, grey body lay cold and inert. But at the touch of Paddy's hand the kitten stirred, moved his head a fraction and tried to mew. He was too weak, and no sound came out. Paddy, tears raining down her face, picked him up with infinite care. He was as light as a cobweb, and that hurt her. All this time, for eleven days, they had been trapped inside the crate. Why, oh why, had she not realized the possibility before? It was heavy enough to muffle their cries—nobody had come near enough to hear. The day the Peytons moved had been rough and windy, just like today. The cats must have bolted terrified from the shed, and hidden beneath the crate, tilted on its side. Then a sudden gust of wind, a crash, and they were

106

imprisoned. It was all so blindingly obvious now.

For Misty—unable, in her loneliness and hunger and despair, to turn to the one person near whom she knew and trusted, it was too late. But, after death, her spirit had lingered, desperately seeking help for her kitten.

'I'll look after him, Misty, I promise,' Paddy said shakily, and solemnly touched Misty's cold wet fur. Then biting her lip, she turned homewards, cradling the kitten beneath her anorak, warm there at last.

Her parents were in the kitchen when she burst in. They stood amazed for a second when they saw what Paddy was carrying. Then her father without a word helped her heat a little milk, and himself added a few drops of brandy. At first the milk ran down the kitten's chin, but after several minutes it stirred, and a tiny red tongue appeared and gave a feeble lick. They got some down its throat, and then laid it on a soft, warm towel near the boiler. Paddy, still kneeling beside the tiny, emaciated animal, turned then and looked at her mother.

'Misty's dead, Mum,' she said, rubbing at the tears and rain on her face.

Her mother gazed back at her in silence, then came over and squeezed her shoulder.

'I'm sorry, love,' she said gently.

'This one will pull through, Paddy. He's young and strong,' said her father, coming to stand beside her. 'He's breathing better now—you see?' He paused, then went on: 'And we'll keep him, if Mrs Peyton doesn't want him, won't we, Jan?' He looked steadily at his wife.

Mrs Bailey opened her mouth to voice her usual objections, looked again at Paddy's wet face, and blew her nose.

'Of course we will,' she said. 'Poor little creature.'

Unbelieving joy lit Paddy's face. 'Oh, can we? Can he be mine?' She leaned over the kitten, touching him gently under the chin, where Misty had always liked to be touched. And, incredibly, the ghost of a purr vibrated from his crumpled little body.

THE SINISTER
SCHOOLMASTER

by Rosemary Timperley

Peter wanted to go to the Comprehensive School because most of his friends in the area were going there. His mother, however, wanted him to go to a small, private school, where he'd get 'individual attention'. His father kept quiet and left mother and son to fight it out.

'I don't want "individual attention",' Peter said. 'I'd rather be one of the mob. I don't mind a bit of roughness, if that's what you're afraid of. If I'm bashed, I can bash back.'

'That,' said his mother, 'is the very attitude I want you to discard. You tend to turn life into a battlefield. This nice little school should make you more gentlemanly.'

Peter gave a voiced imitation of someone being sick.

'Don't be disgusting!' she snapped. 'It's time you were taught some manners.'

'They say on the telly that it's parents that's responsible for their children's manners,' said Peter, 'so if I'm awful it's because of the way I've been upbrung.'

'Brought up,' she corrected him automatically.

'Why?' said Peter. 'You cling, you clung; you ring, you rung; you bring, you brung——'

'You ring, you rang, or you have rung,' she corrected him.

'You ding, you dung,' he muttered.

'*What* did you say?'

'Nothing.'

'I should think so. You start at St. Edmund's tomorrow, Peter, and nothing you can say will make me change my mind.'

'*Saint* Edmund's,' he moaned. 'I expect the Head has long white hair with a halo balanced on top.' But he knew that the battle was lost. His mother was only a woman, but she was tough as old rope when she set her mind on anything, and she wanted her son to be a 'gentleman'. It made you mad. He thought longingly of the state school, where his mates were going, and where some of the teachers even looked like human beings. He was full of gloom when he set out next morning for the first day of term.

He got on the bus, wearing his prissy uniform and carrying a small case with pencils, pens, rubber, compasses and similar daft things. The bus-ride took about fifteen minutes, then, 'Church

110

Road,' the conductor said, and Peter knew that was where he must get off. He alighted, and the friendly old bus trundled away, leaving him alone on the edge of a new world...

It was then that the fog descended. It came down suddenly, cold and grey and blanketing, sending a shiver through him. He had been told which way to walk and now began to plod along a road with tall trees on either side. They were menacing, like sentinels. They watched and whispered. Peter was usually quick enough to be brave and defiant when there was something to defy, but in this blind-making fog all he could do was put one foot in front of the other and grow more and more uneasy.

He suddenly felt *afraid* of this new school.

All the same, he was grateful to see a light at last, though it must be a light from the hated school. Yes, there was a driveway, and a building crouching farther on, with one single golden eye glaring at him. It struck him as odd that there was only one light on in the building. He knew it was a small school, but surely there should be more than one lighted classroom. For the window was that of a classroom, and class had started, so he realised with dismay that he must be late. He could say he was 'delayed by the fog', of course, although he hadn't got lost or anything—had he?

He went closer to the window and looked in.

About a dozen boys sat there, in similar uniforms to his own. That meant he'd found the right school, anyway. The boys sat very attentively. They were pale of face and their eyes were scared. The teacher was at the desk in front of them. He was a short, bull-shouldered man with a red face, white hair, which was long at the sides but left a

111

pink 'halo' of baldness, top-back of his head. He was gesticulating with his right hand and carried something tucked under his left arm, ready for use.

It was a cane.

He asked a boy a question. The boy answered. Peter couldn't hear what was said, but the teacher gave a wolfish smile and beckoned to the boy, who came out to the front and bent over.

The schoolmaster seized the cane in his right hand, raised it, and brought it down crackingly hard on the boy's bottom. He hit him again, and again, and again, and his expression was joyful.

'Stop that!' shouted Peter.

The class froze. The teacher turned towards the window. Pale grey eyes peered into dark grey fog. Then the man marched across and flung open the window. 'Who is that? You—boy—out there—what did you say?'

'I said "Stop that",' Peter answered.

Thick arms, like a couple of little tree-trunks, shot out of the window and grabbed him by the shoulders. He dropped his case on the grass. He struggled. Useless. He was lugged inside. The window was closed again. Peter was dumped on the classroom floor, the man with the cane looming over him.

A terrible stillness seemed to have descended. The boys were quiet and motionless, seeming hardly to breathe. The man stood like a statue of wrath. Peter had to admit to himself that he was very frightened indeed.

Then the silence was broken. 'And who,' asked the sinister schoolmaster, 'are you?'

'Peter Lorrimer.'

'And what are you doing here?'

'I'm a pupil here. It's my first day.'

'Your first day—what?'

'My first day being here.'

'Your first day being here—what?'

'My first day being here at this school.'

'Your first day being here at this school—what?'

'This school called St. Edmund's,' said Peter.

'This school called St. Edmund's—what?'

'A rotten dump!' said Peter, exasperated.

'Stand up!' Peter stood. 'Bend over.' Peter bent. Crack! The cane came down on his bottom.

'Did you enjoy that, Peter Lorrimer?'

'No.'

'No—what?'

'No, I didn't enjoy it!'

Crack came the cane.

'No, you didn't enjoy it—WHAT?' screamed this maniac.

A whisper from the class: 'Ssssay "ssssir".'

Silence for a moment. The fog thickened outside. The oppressiveness of fear thickened too. Peter felt half-paralysed in this nightmare. He was full of pain, yet it was a dead sort of pain, felt yet not felt. Weird.

Now the teacher spoke. 'There is no pupil called Peter Lorrimer in this school. You are an impostor. Why are you wearing our school uniform?'

'I am a pupil—my mother sent me——'

'Your mother sent you—WHAT?'

'SIR!'

Another swish from the cane.

'That's not fair,' said Peter. 'I said "sir".'

'That was for being a liar.'

Swish...

'And that was for arguing about it. Now go and sit at that desk.' Peter obeyed. 'Let's see how much you know, you impostor in the uniform of St. Edmund's, of which I am proud to be Headmaster. I go—I went. I come——' He stopped and waited.

He really is stark raving bonkers, thought Peter. But lunatics must be humoured, so he said hopefully, 'You come, *sir*.'

'The boy is a half-wit. A dunderhead. I come——' Again he waited.

'Thank you for coming,' said Peter, adding a hasty, *sir*.'

'Heaven grant me patience. Listen. I go—I went. I come——'

Light dawned. The silly clot wanted the past

tense of 'come'.

'I came,' said Peter.

'I bring.'

'I brung.'

'You WHAT?'

'I brung, SIR!'

'Brung, brung, brung? Anyone heard the word "brung"?'

A titter of sycophantish laughter from the class.

Peter's conversation with his mother came blessedly back to him. 'I brought,' he said.

'I ring.'

'I rung. No—take that back—I rang, or I have rung. Like you'd say "I rang up" or "I have rung up".'

'I wonder what strange country this boy comes from,' mocked the teacher, 'and what strange language they speak there. Rang up, rung up—what does it mean?'

'It means what it says, sir. Like when you ring someone up, on the telephone.'

'The what?'

'The telephone. *Tele*. As in television, telegram, telecommunications——' His voice faded as the teacher's face turned a deeper shade of crimson.

'Thank you,' said the man. 'Thank you, Peter Lorrimer, for breaking into my class, disturbing my lesson, dressing up in our school uniform, pretending to be a pupil and then talking a lot of gibberish. If there are any words to be invented here, *I* will do the inventing.'

'I'm not inventing anything!'

'You are not inventing anything—WHAT?'

'SIR!'

'Stand up! Bend over!' *Swish, swish, swish* went the cane. In Peter's ears, it seemed to turn into the sound of a raging wind, or a thundering waterfall. His ears would burst!

And it seemed suddenly as if they did. There was a sort of explosion in his head. Light blazed. He found himself lying on the pavement, and people were gathering round him. He supposed that the teacher had beaten him unconscious, then carried him here, bleeding and bruised, for he saw the tall trees which lined the road to the school. The fog had gone.

'He's coming round,' a woman said. 'It's all right, lovey. You're all right now.' She helped him to his feet.

'What happened, old son?' a man asked.

'He was trying to beat me to death,' said Peter. 'He's mad.'

'Kid's been dreaming,' said another voice. 'No signs of damage on him, are there?'

'No. Just a little faint, that's all it was,' said the woman, brushing the pavement dust from his blazer. 'Where do you live?'

Peter told her. One of the men offered to drive him home. He hardly spoke in the car. He felt exhausted. The driver dropped him at his own gate. 'Shall I come in with you?' he offered. 'Will anyone be there?'

'Yes, thank you. My mother's there. Thanks for the lift.'

'You go in and have a good rest,' said the man, and drove off.

Peter let himself into the house. His mother heard him and came into the hall, frowning. 'Oh, Peter, how could you be so naughty?' she said. 'The Headmaster has been on the phone to me—'

'I don't care what he said about me,' Peter said. 'He was horrible and cruel and mad. I'm never

116

going back there. He tried to murder me!' And he poured out the whole story.

His mother listened. His tone was so convincing that she half-believed him. Then she said, 'If you had such a beating, let's see how sore you are.'

'I should think I'll be scarred for life,' said Peter, pulling down his trousers and wondering, as he did so, why his bottom didn't hurt. His mother looked.

'There isn't a mark on you,' she declared. 'Not even the smallest bruise. You've been telling me lies—dangerous lies, too. If you were older, you could be had up for slander for making accusations like that against the Headmaster. And I know for a fact that you did *not* turn up at school at all this morning, because the Head rang up to ask why you hadn't arrived. Oh, Peter, what am I going to do with you when you behave like this? I know you didn't want to go there, but to tell these wicked lies——'

'I wasn't telling lies!' cried Peter. 'It happened! And all in that dreadful fog——'

'There has been no fog—none at all—except in your perverse mind,' she said.

He went very cold. All the indignation died out of him. He whispered: 'If it didn't happen—yet it did—*what* happened? Who was that man with the white hair and the red face, and thick arms and shoulders, and a beastly smile—and a voice which seemed to cut through you, just as the cane did? Who was he?'

'An invented character in your story,' said his mother. 'The Headmaster of St. Edmund's is tall, dark, rather thin and has a very nice smile. I went to see him before I decided to send you there.'

Peter felt dazed and ill. It had all been too much.

You could go on fighting against circumstance for just so long, and then—he broke into tears.

As he melted, so did his mother. She took him in her arms. 'Oh, darling what is all this about?' she said. 'Why did you make up that story? Did you really think I'd believe it?'

'It happened,' wept Peter.

'Where have you really been all morning?'

'Where I said. Then I found myself lying in the street and a man drove me home.'

'What man?'

'I don't know—a nice man—they were all very nice—the passers-by who stopped to pick me up—they were kind—people should always be kind—not like *him*! That—that sinister school-master!'

Even if his home was sometimes a battlefield, his mother now proved a gentle victor. She was so unaccustomed to seeing him cry that she realised something must be badly wrong. She took him up to bed, tucked him in with a hot-water-bottle, kissed him on the forehead and told him to go to sleep. He did sleep, too. Deeply, dream-lessly. It was evening when he woke, blinking con-tentedly in the safety of his own little room. Then his father came in.

'Your mother's been telling me——'

'It all happened, Dad. Honest!'

His father sat on the end of the bed. 'We know now that you went to the school, Peter, although no one saw you there. Your case was found outside one of the classroom windows.'

'That's right,' said Peter. 'I dropped it when that dreadful Headmaster dragged me inside.'

'No one dragged you inside,' said his father. 'Your mother did wonder if there could be something in your story, as you were so upset, so she went to the school this afternoon. She thought maybe one of the teachers was like the man you'd described. No one there is even remotely like him. No one there *now*, that is.'

'No one there *now*?' Peter echoed.

'The Head, Mr Rennick, has come to see you. He wants to talk to you about it.' He went to fetch the other man, and Peter waited. If that villain with the cane walked in——

A tall, dark, anxious-faced man came in and closed the door behind him. He had a book under his arm, not a cane. 'Hello, Peter. I'm Mr Rennick, the Headmaster of St. Edmund's.'

'Then who was the man with white hair?' Peter asked.

'Ever heard of John Bashman, nicknamed "Old Basher"?' Mr Rennick asked him. Peter shook his head. 'Here's a picture of him.' Mr Rennick opened the book, called *History of St. Edmund's School*, and displayed a full-page illustration. It was a reproduction of the portrait of a man, in colour. A white-haired, red-faced thick-bodied man, It was labelled: 'John Bashman, the First Headmaster.'

'That's him,' said Peter. 'That's the man who beat me.'

'That man has been dead for a hundred years. He wasn't nicknamed "Old Basher" for nothing. He caned the pupils for the smallest misdemeanour. He was a sadistic bully, to my mind, but in those days beatings in school were more common than they are now. It was an age of violence. Now your story is that you looked through the classroom window and saw him there; that he dragged you inside, and so on——'

'He did! In that awful fog!'

'There was no fog. It was a bright morning. The teacher who spent all morning in that classroom was taking physics. It's a lab, rather than an ordinary classroom. You realise now, don't you? You had some sort of dream-awake. A hallucination of some kind.'

'You mean I saw ghosts of the past,' Peter said calmly. 'That would be why he'd never heard of the telephone or television. He said I was talking gibberish and that if anyone was going to invent words, he would do it.'

'It was all a dream, Peter. You never wanted to come to my school. You were resentful about it. Your mother says you dashed out without any breakfast, so you were empty. You got to the school, couldn't face going in, dumped your case, fled back to the road—and then you fainted. Overwrought nerves. While unconscious, you had this dream. Does that make sense to you?'

'I suppose so. But it must have been more than an ordinary dream, as Old Basher really did exist.'

'Yes. And I expect you'd read about him somewhere and forgotten. What the conscious mind forgets, the unconscious retains. That's my explanation. It makes more sense than "ghosts". There are no such things.' He spoke confidently, almost arrogantly.

He wouldn't be so cocky about it if *he'd* had Old Basher standing over him with that cane, Peter thought—and, suddenly, behind the Headmaster's shoulder, he saw a shadow forming...

The shadow gained colour and solidity. It seemed to have sprung in some curious way from the illustration in the open book, which Mr Rennick had placed on a shelf behind him. There was

120

the white hair, the red face, the thick body—the raised arm with the cane in it—the curling smile—the pale eyes, glaring at the back of the Headmaster's head. 'Imposter!' spat the lips—or that could have been the sound of rain falling on the leaves in the garden. The arm with the cane was raised higher——

'Look out!' screamed Peter. 'Old Basher is just behind you! He's going to wallop you!'

As the cane descended, Mr Rennick gave a cry, and the light went out. Peter went right down under the bedclothes, in case Old Basher started on him next.

A few moments later, the bedclothes were pulled away from him. His mother was bending over him. The room was dimly lit by light from the passage. His father was outlined in the doorway. Mr Rennick was rubbing his head.

'It's all right, Peter,' his mother was saying. 'The electric bulb fell out of its socket and hit poor Mr Rennick on the head. That's why the light went out.' She turned to the Headmaster. 'My fault, that. I couldn't have fixed it properly when I put it in the other day.'

'I've always told you to leave that sort of job to me,' Peter's father said irritably. 'Sorry about this, Mr Rennick. Come downstairs and have a drink.'

The two men departed, but before he left the room, Mr Rennick gave Peter a long, suspicious look.

Now his mother fussed over him a little and he lay down to sleep. Strangely, he no longer felt afraid of Old Basher, who had so obviously had it in for Mr Rennick rather than himself. Resented anyone else taking over the school, even a hundred years afterwards. That would be it. Peter did, how-

121

ever, feel a little afraid of the look Mr Rennick had given him. When he went to St. Edmund's, there wouldn't be any beating or cruelty, but he wouldn't be popular. The Head definitely didn't like or trust him. Oh, life could be hell sometimes. It really could. He slept.

In the morning, his mother brought him breakfast in bed.

'You're going to stay at home today,' she said, 'then your father and I will arrange for you to go to the Comprehensive.'

'Wow!' He nearly hit the ceiling with relieved delight.

'Peter, be careful, you'll spill your tea.'

'What made you change your mind?' he asked her.

'I didn't,' she said, rather grimly. 'Mr Rennick changed his. He said he didn't want you at the school. He said some neurotic children cause outbreaks of poltergeist activity, and he didn't want the pleasant atmosphere of St. Edmund's disturbed. He struck me as pretty neurotic himself,' she added. 'What a fuss to make over a falling light-bulb! As if *you* could possibly have been responsible for that.'

It was Old Basher, thought Peter. Clever old ghost!

Then his father descended upon him. 'Enjoying your breakfast and the "good news"?' he said sardonically. 'You cunning little devil! You were determined to get your own way, weren't you? Tell me—how did you wangle that poltergeist effect?'

'I didn't,' Peter began. 'It was Old——' Then he stopped. It would be no use telling his father the truth. He had a sceptical nature, limited, lacking in imagination. Still, he wasn't a bad sort. Peter

122

smiled. His father winked and departed.

In fact Peter felt friendly towards everyone this morning. Even Old Basher. Especially Old Basher! But for him, Peter would have had to go to St Edmund's...

'Thank you,' he said, impulsively and aloud—and an echo in the air—or maybe it was only the gurgling of a water-pipe—said: 'Thank you—WHAT?' and Peter bellowed back: 'SIR!'

SPOOKY STORIES No. 2
Edited by Barbara Ireson;
illustrated by Les Matthews

These chilling tales of the strange and supernatural invite you
to:

Join a race that can never be won with a headless horse and
its headless rider...

Meet the phantom of a great black dog with murder in its
past...

Discover the ghostly secret of an ancient deed box...

Hear the curious tale of Father Aethelwulf and the dragon
he met on a train...

Eight icy tales featuring ghosts and bewitchment of the animal
world...

0   552   52104   3   65p

SPOOKY STORIES No. 3
Edited by Barbara Ireson;
illustrated by Carolyn Bull

A further selection of seven spine-chilling tales and unspeakable horrors is unravelled by master storytellers of the ghostly and supernatural:

Read of the child ghost determined to prove her innocence beyond death...

Pale with terror as the shadowy Whistlers close in on the finder of a witch's bottle and its unearthly brew...

Beware of innocent Hallowe'en games and looking into a mirror on that tormented night...

Shake in your shoes with two young hikers as a deserted mining village is suddenly peopled around and *through* them...

0 552 52140 X   85p

KINGS, GHOSTS AND HIGHWAYMEN
Josephine Poole;
illustrated by Barbara Swiderska

Pippenhay, with its dry rot, Tudor plumbing and resident Aunt
Millicent—when Giles and Alice Dory moved down from
London with the children, Charlotte and Vincent, even the cat
slumped into gloomy despair.

But as their first year rolled by and Pippenhay blossomed once
more, Charlotte and Vincent soon met friends, villagers and
relations eager to tell them thrilling tales of their west country
home and ancestors, and about the countryside they explored.

There were legends, folklore, old wives' tales and strange
customs—stories of white witches and spellbindings, of fairy
fairs seen over the hill, of wedding dancers turned to stone,
of kings, queens and saints, princes and princesses, and highwaymen who stole the ladies' hearts along with their jewels . . .

0   552   52137   X   95p

THE BEST OF SHADOWS
Adapted from the Thames Television series SHADOWS
illustrated by Les Matthews

Lurking among the SHADOWS are strange tales of the weird
and wonderful, the magic and the supernatural to thrill your
imagination.

Seven chilling tales including such mysteries as the ancient
omen of a skull-headed Horn Dance; the ghostly echoes of a
death caught in the webs of time; the sad curse of a crippled
dancer; each told by a master storyteller—Joan Aiken—
Josephine Poole—Ewart Alexander and many more.

0   552   52096   9   65p

If you would like to receive a newsletter telling you about our new children's books, fill in the coupon with your name and address and send it to:

Gillian Osband,

Transworld Publishers Ltd,

Century House,

61–63 Uxbridge Road, Ealing,

London, W5 5SA

Name ....

Address ....

....

CHILDREN'S NEWSLETTER

All the books on the previous pages are available at your bookshop or can be ordered direct from Transworld Publishers Ltd., Cash Sales Dept. P.O. Box 11, Falmouth, Cornwall.

Please send full name and address together with cheque or postal order—no currency, and allow 45p per book to cover postage and packing (plus 20p each for additional copies).